Tales of The Witching Hour

By T.H. Cini

Copyright © 2020 T.H. Cini.

All rights reserved. No part of this publication may be reproduced, distributed, or transmitted in any form or by any means, including photocopying, recording, or other electronic or mechanical methods, without the prior written permission of the publisher, except in the case of brief quotations embodied in critical reviews and certain other noncommercial uses permitted by copyright law.

ISBN: 979-8555043641 (Paperback)

For Georgia

Tales of The Witching Hour

By T.H. Cini

Index

Part 1: The Man in the Fedora Hat........................ Page 6

Part 2: The Red Balloon .... Page 63

Part 3: The Typewriter ....…......... Page 100

Part 4: The Whispering Room .... Page 141

Part 1

The Man in the Fedora Hat

Friday, April 27, 1984, 3:00 a.m.

Tick, tick, tick, tick . . . I heard as I slowly opened my eyes. It was dark in my room. *It must be the middle of the night.* I turned on my lamp and grab the clock from my night table. 3:00 a.m. Exactly three in the morning. Another sleepless night. I put the clock back and closed my eyes. *Just go to sleep. Think of lovely things to fall asleep to. How about the ocean? The sound of ocean waves as they come and go and splash against the beach with the moonlight in the distance. Or maybe the pretty lady I saw at the supermarket; her blouse open just enough to see her soft skin and the beginning of where her breast starts. No, that's not going to work. Back to the ocean waves crashing, splashing against the beach. The waves, the splash . . . the crash* tick, tick, tick, tick. My eyes opened again.

I grabbed the clock. It was made by the Shanghai Diamond company, and this one I'd had since I was a young boy. The face of the clock was a night sky with stars in the background. The second hand was a meteor-like object which moved around the clock face. If you held it under the light for ten minutes, it glowed in the dark while you fell asleep watching it go around and around. I'd stared at that meteor-like object many times as I fell asleep as a boy.

Damn! Another sleepless night! This had been happening all week. I thought I'd be exhausted from waking up in the middle of the night, but there I was. 3:00 a.m. Friday morning. I slid out of bed, took a sip of water that I placed on my night table every night, and pushed myself up so that I could peer out the window. I pulled open the right drape to see, as usual, a row of houses and beyond that, the wet pavement of John Street. My house was on an elevated road, and from my bedroom window, I had a full view of the row of houses with their backyards along John Street. On the other side, was a ravine. From my window, I had a clear view of the sidewalk, the grass lane, and the pavement, due to the way the neighborhood was designed in the 1950s. John Street wasn't very busy. There was a large ruddy rock on the grass lane that I thought was beautifully sculptural. While I stood at the window for a few minutes, there was something peaceful about how undramatic and lifeless the street was in the middle of the night.

I closed the drape, returned to my bed, took another sip of water, and lay down.

Saturday, April 28, 1984, 3:06 a.m.

Please, let it be morning. Please! I opened my eyes and turned on the lamp. Six after three in the morning. Damn! I turned the light off and closed my eyes. I tried all the tricks I was told would help one fall asleep; counting backward from 100 and counting sheep. *Ugh! This is frustrating.* I got up, sat on my bed, rubbed my face with my hands, and took a sip of water. I stood, walked towards my window, pulled the right drape open, and looked outside.

A man stood on John Street beside the big rock. I rubbed my eyes to make sure I wasn't seeing things. Yes, a man was standing beside the big rock on the grass lane as if he were waiting for someone or something. He wore what looked like a fedora hat and a full suit. He held a piece of luggage or maybe a briefcase, though it appeared to be too large for a briefcase from where I could see. The man stood almost motionless, facing toward the ravine. I stayed at my window watching him, wondering if someone had put a mannequin on the side of the road as a joke. He brought up his left arm to look at his watch. *Ahh . . . it is a real man.* I let go of the drape and made my way back to my bed and sat for a moment, pondering the thought of opening a book. *That might help me sleep.* From outside I heard the sound of a bus coming up the street and then stopped. The man was obviously waiting for transportation. After a few moments, I heard the driver release the brakes and its engine run down the street, fading into the distance.

No, I don't want to read. I don't know what I will do. Maybe I will count sheep. Yes, try that. It's childish, but I'll try anything. I tried closing my eyes, but the streetlights poked through the drapes, and I realized that they didn't close properly, letting in more light than I would like. I got up to fix it and checked outside again. To my surprise, the man was still there! Weird. I was sure I heard a bus stop on that street. *Maybe he is waiting for someone and the bus mistook him for a passenger waiting to be picked up.* I watched for a minute but felt exhausted, so made my way back to bed and counted sheep. One sheep . . . two sheep . . . three sheep . . . four sheep . . .

Sunday, April 29, 1984, 3:21 a.m.

Tick, tick, tick, tick . . . My eyes opened to see darkness. I reached for the clock. 3:21 in the morning. *It's Sunday. Just go back to sleep.*

I put the clock back on the table, rolled onto my back, and gazed up at the ceiling. The stream of light poked between the top of my drapes and the window frame. The streetlights weren't bright, but I could feel the strength of its glow as it broke through my window.

"What is it that keeps waking me up at 3:00 a.m.?" I asked aloud, still facing the ceiling.

I sat up. The glow from the streetlights peeked through the entire perimeter of the window. I opened the right drape to see the man in the fedora hat standing in the same spot he was yesterday, but this time there was someone with him. A man: a young man with blue jeans and a black jacket sitting on the rock while the man in the fedora hat remained by the road.

The man with the hat held the same suitcase and again wore a suit. I waited for a moment. He didn't appear to talk to the man in the black jacket and on occasion checked his watch. My clock ticked away on my nightstand and the streetlights illuminated the room as I held the drape open while the two men began to engage in a conversation. The young man sitting on the rock appeared to even laugh and seemed very relaxed. The man with the hat seemed quite serious from where I was standing and didn't turn his head to face the other. The conversation seemed to stop, and the young man looked down the road as if he were waiting for something.

I tired from looking at the two men. I let the drape close, sat, and took a sip of my water. I lifted my feet and shoved them under the covers. *Maybe counting the spots on my ceiling will help. One, two, three.*

I heard the sound of the bus coming up the street again, and it stopped. Then after a few seconds, the bus released its brakes and drove off. I waited for a minute and then had this overwhelming feeling of wanting to look out again. I slid back out of bed and pulled the drape open to spy the man with the fedora hat still standing. The other was gone. Why would a man wait at a bus stop and not take the bus? Two nights in a row! *He must get picked up by a friend later.* What an odd time to be waiting for a bus. I didn't know they ran through the night.

He stayed so still that I wondered if he was lost. I had the urge to put some clothes on and ask him, but the feeling of exhaustion came over me, which I welcomed after nights of sleeplessness. I let the drape drop to close out the light. I pulled my clock closer and watched the meteor tick around the night sky as I fell asleep. Tick, tick, tick, tick, tick . . .

Monday, April 30, 1984, 3:00 a.m.

Bing! *Here we go again.* I reached for my clock. Right on time. 3:00 a.m. sharp! I sat up and rubbed my face with both hands as if I was waking up for the day. This had become so routine. I felt like I should just get up, but there was nothing to do but wait until work. *I'll be too tired if I try and stay up. What to do. What to do.*

I lifted my head out of my hands. The glowing light peeked from the perimeter of my window. I pulled the drape open. There he was. The man with the hat, standing in the same spot as the previous night, beside the rock. What could he possibly be waiting for at 3:00 a.m.?

"Ok. Enough is enough," I said, grabbing a pair of pants and a sweater. "I'm going to see if he is real."

I put a light jacket over my sweater, grabbed a pair of shoes, and tip-toed down the stairs. Once I got to the front door, I slipped them on quickly and left. Once outside I could feel the chilly moisture in the air. I could see the faint fog from my breath as I cornered my street onto John Street. I slowed my pace to appear that I was casual. The man remained. As I came closer, he didn't acknowledge my footsteps at all. A creepiness came over me. It almost felt like I was approaching a ghost. I felt anxious. My heart raced. He still didn't turn his head, so I sat on the rock. The man wore a dark brown suit while holding a suitcase in his right hand. His left arm hung along his side. The hat created a shadow over his face, which hid his features.

"Hello."

The man with the fedora hat turned slowly toward me and nodded. "Hello."

"Silly question," I said, with a half-grin. "Are you waiting for a bus?"

"Indeed, I am," he answered, still facing ahead.

I pondered for a moment how I could get more from him without coming across as nosy.

"Do you know what time it comes?"

"Anytime, now."

What shall I ask? Nothing came to mind. I scanned the street and up the hill to where my house was and then up and down John Street. There wasn't a noise, except the distant splashing of the stream down the ravine. I felt I was on another planet and this man and I were the only souls on it: just him and me.

I sat there almost stunned, wondering what I was even doing there and if this conversation was even real. With my back towards him, I thought, *I can just imagine, that when I turn around, the man with the hat will be gone. This is all a dream.* I slowly turned around. He was *still* there. What are you going to do?

At that moment, I heard the faint roar of a vehicle coming up the south end of John Street. The man in the hat faced down the road, and I got up from the rock. I could see the headlights in the distance approach us: a bus. It slowed down and stopped in front of where we stood. The bus sat idle for a moment. The man didn't move towards it, and the driver didn't open the doors.

Bizarre.

There didn't seem to be anyone in it, but the windows were dark and appeared to be fogged up from the inside. It didn't seem that he was going to board the bus, so instead, *I* approached the vehicle. When the doors opened, I felt an overwhelming pressure from inside and found it difficult to breathe. The driver wore a uniform and a hat. He was heavy set but I couldn't make out his face. It was as if my vision was impaired when peering into the bus from the outside.

I backed up, but the man in the fedora hat remained motionless. The driver closed the doors, released the brakes, and went on his way. The taillights diminished as it drove over the hill toward the other end of town.

"Why didn't you take the bus?" I asked.

"That's not my bus."

"I see." Confused.

After I sat back on the rock, an intoxicating feeling came over me, and I felt the urge to fall asleep. I didn't want to go. But I had to. My exhaustion took over.

"I'm going to go now," I said to the figure in front of me. "It was nice to meet you."

"Good night, son," he said without turning his head.

I headed towards my house.

Tuesday, May 1, 1984, 3:01 am

Right on time. I quickly got out of bed and made my way to the window. He was there all right, but he had company. There was what appeared to be an elderly lady with a large flower design on her dress which puffed out. She was a larger woman talking the man with the hat's ear off. I grabbed my jacket and shoes, made my way down the stairs, and set off to see the two.

"Oh," she said as she noticed me approaching them. "Another passenger. Isn't this nice?" She spoke in a jolly voice as I sheepishly approached.

"Hello again, son," the man in the hat said as he nodded.

"Oh! You know this young man?" she asked with a surprised expression.

The man nodded in acknowledgment.

"And where will you be off to?" she asked me.

"Pardon me?"

"Where will the bus be taking you?"

"I'm not taking the bus anywhere ma'am."

"Oh. That's odd." She said with a confused look on her face. She turned to the man in the hat. "What about you, sir?"

"I'm going to see a young lady." I could see the smile grow from underneath the shadow from the brim of his hat.

"Oh my. Well good for you!" She said as she slapped her hand on his chest. "Oh, I'm sorry." Her face changed: her jolliness quickly disappeared. She studied his face. Something was running through her mind.

"I get the feeling that your bus may not be coming tonight if you don't mind me saying."

"I'll wait," he replied quite calmly. "I'm a patient man."

"Hmmm . . . yes. You must be." She expressed with a certain reservation in her tone.

"Would you like to know where I'm going to?" she asked, quite jolly again. "I'm going to see my family."

She glanced down at her hand, with her purse strung on her left forearm. "My oldest brother -- Harold, my aunt Emma and Uncle Bob, my little sister Jeannette and my husband George." She took a deep sigh. "Oh, it's been so long. I can't wait!" she said, distracted by gazing down the street. "When is the bus coming?" she asked her voice tense.

"It should be here anytime," the man in the hat replied.

"Hmmm." Her eyes bounced back and forth between me and the man in the hat.

"You two seem like an odd pair. Are you friends?"

"One could say that," he answered before I could think of how I would have answered the question.

"Are you close to your family?" she asked me.

Being caught off guard with now her second direct question, I struggled to answer it. "Well . . . yes."

"I'm sorry for my being so blunt. It's the way I was raised. The reason why I ask, young man, is that you may be taking your family for granted. I know I did when I was younger." She paused and looked up to the sky. "I remember despising my father for being so protective. I wanted my freedom but didn't know what to do with it, you see. I had a crush on a boy, a neighbor. And, although he was quite handsome, I knew very little about him. Anyway, I wanted to go to a dance, and I know the boy was going to be there and made a fuss about not having to go with a chaperone. After I pled with my parents, my father allowed me to go without him coming along. Well, I got my way and went to the dance with one of my girlfriends. I was giving this boy the eye all night long and near the end of the evening, he grabbed me to dance. Once I became close to him, there was an evilness in his eyes that I didn't notice before, and it had also occurred to me that he had been drinking.

"He became very rough with me while dancing and asked if I would like to step outside with him. At this point, I was not enjoying the boy's company or the dancing and wanted nothing more than to go home. After the song ended, he grabbed my arm and headed for the outside doors. I felt embarrassed and afraid of what might happen as he began to overpower me, and my girlfriend was nowhere in sight.

"At that very moment, this young man came between us to stop him. It was Harold," she said with a lilt. "My brother, Harold. Out of nowhere. There he was. Do you know what?" she asked me with excitement in her voice and her eyes wide open. "My father sent Harold to the dance to watch over me and make sure I got home safely. Harold told me that father's wish was for him to be inconspicuous, but present. And till this day . . ." she said, with her eyes beginning to fill up, "I still remember that family is the most important. Out of the hundreds of people that were at that dance, it ended up being my family that looked after me. From that day on, I have never taken my family for granted. Sure, we have upset one another here and there, but family will always be there for you. Remember that. I've had friends come and go, and I've come across many acquaintances." She paused. "Your family will always be there for you."

Down the road, I could hear the sound of the bus. The man in the hat and the woman seemed compelled towards the sound as it became closer. The woman held her purse close to her waist. The bus stopped, and she stepped closer. After a moment, the bus doors opened. The woman angled toward me and waved goodbye, turning back around to board the bus. I returned the wave.

The man in the hat didn't move. I stepped towards the bus doors to have another peek inside. This time, I could smell the sweet scent of some kind, like a flower from an exotic rainforest. I knew it was the same driver as before but still couldn't see his face. The doors closed and the driver slowly accelerated up John Street.

Wednesday, May 2, 1984, 3:07 a.m.

I pulled the drape open to see the man in the hat waiting for his bus. I let the drape close, but before I got dressed to go and meet him, I sat on my bed and thought for a moment: *why is he not getting on that bus? How did that woman know that that wasn't his bus? Who is this man? How come I've never heard the bus in the middle of the night before? I must go into town, check the city transit commission and see when this route started -- not that it would matter much.* I got up, grabbed my jacket and shoes, and out I went.

"Hello, sir."

"Hello, son," he said, perusing the ravine. "Do you know that there are voices in that ravine?"

"Pardon me?"

"Yes. I hear them once in a while. You should go and listen. I think it may be of some importance to you."

"What would anyone want to be doing in there at this time of night?" I was quite perplexed.

"You may not see them, but they are there. Go across and listen for yourself."

Curiosity came over me, much like when I peeked inside the bus the previous night. I glanced at the ravine and then back to the man in the hat.

"I'm going to go." I stepped on the pavement and instantly felt a disturbing tightness in my chest, as I struggled to breathe. I stopped and looked back.

"Go ahead," he urged reassuringly.

The ravine was dense, so heavily treed that I could hear the stream down inside it but couldn't see it. I crossed the street and stepped onto the sidewalk, where I stood for a moment. I didn't hear anything, so I turned back toward the man standing on the other side. I didn't go any farther, as I was fearful, and the tightness in my chest remained.

"Young man," a voice called out to me from beyond the bushes.

I froze in my steps, my heart racing.

"You! Young man," the voice said again.

"Yes?" I replied with a trembling voice.

"Come sit under the lamp post, please."

Up the street, a little farther was a streetlamp with a cement base, which I sat on. I scanned the bushes.

"Do not look for me. It would be better if you listened."

I couldn't tell if the man in the hat was looking at me or not from across the street. I peered down at the sidewalk in front of me where the light cast my shadow.

"What did that man tell you about us here in the ravine?"

The voice was neither male nor female. It had a whisper-like sound, that wasn't frightful, but not warm either.

"He told me that there are voices in the ravine but didn't say much else."

"I see. And you believed him?"

"I had to find out for myself."

"Ahh, how daring of you. Why didn't you come inside the forest, into the ravine?"

I hesitated to answer the question.

"No need to answer."

My chest felt tight with anxiety.

"Young man. I must ask you a question. It will help me better understand you."

"OK."

"Have you ever been in love?"

"No."

"Ahh. And why is that? You are a young man but not young enough to never have felt love. Are you afraid?" the voice asked.

"No." I lied. "Perhaps I am," I then blurted out.

"Hmm. There is so much for you to experience," the voice said. "May I offer you something? A sort of . . . gift?"

"A gift?" I thought it seemed an odd thing for a voice to offer.

"Close your eyes for me."

I did.

"Good."

I waited as I embraced complete darkness within my covered eyeballs, expecting something to appear after the voice told me to open my eyes. I waited on and on. Almost opening my eyes from impatience, I began to feel a warm, tingling sensation in the middle of my chest.

"Do you feel it?"

"I do," I said, completely smiling.

I felt an overwhelming desire to giggle. I had to push it down it was so strong, but it felt wonderful.

"Keep your eyes closed."

While I was feeling this incredible sensation, I could see someone. With my eyes still closed, I could see the image of a woman. Although I could not see her face, her appearance pleased me. She had brown hair and brown eyes, but I still couldn't see her. Even so, it made me happy. When she spoke, it made that warm tingling in my chest become greater. I could feel myself glow.

"That's love," the voice said.

"It's beautiful."

"You can open your eyes now young man. Come back tomorrow. I will have more for you."

"Yes. Yes, I will come back."

I pushed myself off the lamppost base and made my way to the other side of the street towards the man in the hat. I was so looking forward to telling him what I just felt.

As I came closer to the other side, the warm tingling feeling faded. Once I was completely across, the feeling was entirely gone.

I suddenly felt empty. That wonderful sensation had gone. My walk towards the man in the hat had come to a snail's pace, as I was almost embarrassed to tell him. It was like I had found a silver dollar, put it in my pocket with a hole in it, and had to explain how I lost it.

I sat on the rock and looked down at the ground, soaking it all in until a sudden heaviness came over me. I knew I must get to bed. *The bus never came for the man in the hat that night.*

Thursday, May 3, 1984, 3:05 a.m.

I woke with an incredible rush of anticipation regarding what the voice had in store for me that night. I grabbed my jacket and shoes as usual and made my way out of the house. As I descended the hill towards the street, a fearfulness crept up on me. I had forgotten to open the drape to see if the man in the hat was even there. Maybe he'd finally caught his bus and would be gone.

As I rounded the corner, I saw him. Yes indeed, he was there, but he had the company of two: a woman and a young girl. The young girl was speaking to the woman, but I couldn't hear what she was saying as I was too far away.

As I came closer, the young girl stopped to peer up at me.

"Hello."

"Hello," I replied

"Are you waiting for the bus too?"

"Umm," I hesitated, not knowing what to say. "No. I just . . . came for a walk."

"My auntie came to bring me to the bus. Isn't that nice?" She glinted her teeth at me.

"Yes, it is. Where are you and your auntie going to?"

"She's not coming on the bus with me. She's just staying until the bus comes to pick me up."

Her aunt, wearing a large clumsy sun hat, stood beside the man still holding his suitcase. Her aunt hovered over the girl and nodded to me, but I couldn't make out the expression on her face.

"Would you like to know where I'm going now?" the little girl asked.

"Yes, please."

All this time, the man in the hat stood looking out at the road for the bus.

"I have to tell you a story first." She took a deep breath. "My daddy bought me a butterfly catcher for my birthday. I waited and waited for a long, long time to find a butterfly, and then one day, there it was, fluttering its wings in the backyard. It first landed on a tree branch, then on Mommy's rose bush. Once it left the rose bush, it flew away into our neighbor's yard, when I caught it!" she said, holding her two arms to her chest as if she just won a prize. "I kept the netting shut to keep it from flying away. I ran over to my daddy and asked him to get my cage to keep the butterfly in, so he did.

"I kept him on my windowsill, watching him when I woke up, and said goodnight before bedtime. Yesterday, Daddy had to leave for a business trip. Mommy went with him, and my butterfly kept me company while I stayed with Auntie. In the evening . . ." She paused briefly. "I know it was early evening because I just had a peanut butter and jelly sandwich Auntie made for me. Anyway, I felt very sleepy, so Auntie put me to bed, and I asked to have my butterfly beside me while I fell asleep. I woke up in the night and found the cage open, and so was my bedroom window. My butterfly had flown away."

"I'm sorry."

"I cried, and Auntie came to my room. I got dressed and so did Auntie."

"I see," I responded, a little confused.

"That's why Auntie brought me here, to this bus stop, to find my butterfly!" she exclaimed.

Where would that young girl be going at this time of night? What an awful time to wake a young girl to catch a bus.

The girl paced back to her aunt and stood in front while the woman turned down the street in search of the bus. I sat on the rock, contemplating when to cross the road and discover what the voice had in store for me. I was a little anxious but I was drawn to what was next as the previous night felt amazing. I couldn't hear the stream though I'd heard it plainly the night before. It was cooler this night. The air was heavy, as I could see my breath. I thought about the sensation I felt. For a moment, I forgot about the man and the aunt, and the young girl.

At that moment the bus came up the street.

"Here it is, Auntie!" said the young girl, jumping up and down. Still holding her aunt's hand, she situated herself at the end of the curb as the bus approached.

The man regarded the bus as it came but stood perfectly still.

The bus doors opened, and the familiar sweet odor emanated from them. The windows were filled with condensation. I observed the silhouettes of the other passengers as they shifted.

I moved towards the bus to get a better view as the young girl boarded. The bus driver shook his head discreetly, signaling me not to continue, so I stopped.

"Goodbye, Auntie!" The girl turned to wave.

Her aunt waved back, watching as the bus drove away until it was out of sight and then perambulated down the street. I sat on the rock, surrounded by gathering fog as the woman with the large hat faded into it.

I didn't say anything to him about not boarding the bus, as it obviously wasn't the right one. I must admit, I felt a little sorry for him. I don't know why, but I did.

I couldn't wait any longer.

"I'm going to go across the street again."

"OK."

"I stepped onto the pavement, and once again, an odd feeling came over me. I was nervous, but not scared. There was a heaviness in my chest, but it wasn't painful. I reached the lamp post, sat on it as I had the previous night, and waited for the voice.

"I see you've returned." Before I could answer, it continued, "Come into the bushes."

I hesitated as my initial intuition was that I could have been lured into something dangerous or unpleasant.

"Come. Don't be afraid. The gift I gave you last night was a taste, but you need to truly feel it without others around.

I pushed off the lamp post and went to the bush.

"Where do I enter?"

"Right in front of you. Use your hands and arms to push the bushes aside. Close your eyes so as not to scratch them."

I wanted more from this voice. I pushed through the dense bush. The tiny branches scratched my hands, but my coat protected my arms. I closed my eyes tight to not scratch them and kept moving forward. My face was getting scratched, so I placed my hands over, moving through the bushes faster.

Finally, I felt no more resistance from the branches. When I reached the other side, I opened my eyes, but to my surprise, I did not see a stream, grass, trees, or anything like a ravine. I was in what appeared to be a desert with the sun about to rise! I scanned my new surroundings from left to right: nothing but smooth desert-like starkness with a mild glow in the horizon. There was no breeze, no wind, and no odor.

"Do not be afraid. You must trust me."

"OK," I said, but I was trembling.

"Come into the center. Over there." It was said with such clarity that I knew where the voice intended so I entered the center; the center of what, I am not sure, but once I sat, I had a 360-degree view of the horizon: a dull yellow-orange glow, as if the sun were to come up, but from which side? The air seemed rich, as I only needed small breaths to fill my lungs with oxygen. I held my hand in front of my mouth to try and discern my breath, but I couldn't.

"Close your eyes."

I did.

I waited.

Nothing was happening, but I kept my eyes closed. I couldn't hear or smell anything. The silence and darkness were not unnerving. I felt very alone but was not intimidated by it.

I lost patience.

I could wait no more and opened my eyes.

There was an image of a moving entity hovering in front of me. It had no face or recognizable body but more of an energy shifting and changing colors as it moved. It didn't scare me, but it was too difficult to follow, causing me to close my eyes again. I still felt no fear, even with my eyes closed as this energy hovered around me. It moved closer as if it could go right through me. I expected it to hit my chest, but at that very moment, the sensation was not in my chest as it was the night before. Instead, it began in my fingertips on my right hand. I stretched out my arm and could sense its touch from the palm of my hand up to my forearm which sent shivers through me.

I started to drift farther from where I was placed. I felt the horizon in the distance disappear. My body rose as the touching sensation moved from my arm to my chest, and my neck, and then up to my lips. I gave way to it, and let the energy caress me. I needed it. I wanted it. I could not see anything. I didn't need to see anything. I saw no face, but it was there with me.

A sweet smell presented itself, followed by the presence of moisture as if being kissed on the lips. The sensation continued down my neck. The sweet aroma made me feel excited. I wanted more as impatience came over me, but it was met with continuous caressing, for which I gave in once again.

I saw hair flowing back and forth over soft skin. I still could not make out a clear face, but I knew it was the woman from the night before. Tears filled my eyes with pleasure. I let out a deep sigh and felt the breath of the energy brush past my cheek. The incredible sensation was almost too much, at which point it slowly eased, but I was happy, as my pleasure threshold was exceeded, and I needed a withdrawal of it. I lay there, relaxed, the sensation slowly fading. I could hear my breathing and felt the moisture of my expiration as it hit the side of my arm. I tried to take in everything that had just happened. The weight of my body became apparent as I felt the ground beneath me.

A sort of panic came over me when I realized the energy had disappeared. I opened my eyes. I was no longer in the desert but lying on the ground between the dense bushes. The panic changed to sadness as it had the night before. I got up and made my way back towards the street where I then crawled out of the bushes and onto the sidewalk. The man stood beside the street, still waiting for the bus. I felt I had been gone for some time and looked up at the night sky to see if the sun was about to come out, but that wasn't the case.

I expected the voice to say something about my visit, perhaps a parting comment: nothing but silence. I brushed the dirt and leaves off my jacket and pants and crossed the street to where the man in the hat was standing. I sat on the large rock.

"Did you have a nice visit?" the man in the hat asked, still looking out at the road.

"Yes, I did."

Then from nowhere, I bust out with a laugh.

The man in the hat turned his head towards me but didn't say anything, then turned back to the street.

I don't know what came over me at that moment, but I felt a sudden rush of excitement recollecting the physical and emotional pleasure that came from the entity. I felt the laugh come up again, but I concealed it and covered my mouth in embarrassment about doing it again.

I wanted to return immediately to experience what I had just felt. Then, I recalled the previous night and how that felt. It was so different and so beautiful. I wanted to feel both again. There was so much of life I had yet to live.

I peered up. I couldn't see any stars or clouds. There was no breeze either. Unusual.

Down the street where the young girl's aunt had gone, there was only the fog. On the other side, the fog slowly rolled in as well.

I felt sorry for the man because I knew that the bus would not be coming for him that night either.

"May I ask you a question, sir?"

"Go ahead, son," he replied without looking.

"When your bus does come for you," I hesitated slightly. "Where will it be taking you?"

The man didn't reply right away.

"Honestly. . ." He hesitated. "I don't quite know." I couldn't help but feel sorrier for him. What happened across the street in the ravine seemed a distant memory as reality for me was sitting on a rock talking to a man who did not know where he was going.

My legs felt numb. When I got up from the rock, they were wobbly with fatigue. I decided I must get back home as I was feeling a little faint.

"Goodnight, sir. Your bus will come soon."

The man in the hat turned his head slightly and waved.

Friday, May 4, 1984, 3:16 a.m.

I let the drape drop back after seeing the man in the hat still waiting for the bus at the curb.

I definitely had some jump in my step as I walked down the hill. The last two nights were incredible. I felt like a new man. The thought of what the voice may have for me that night and the anticipation that came with it made my heart pump with delight.

As I approached the man, a sort of sadness came over me. I was having these wonderful experiences, but he was sort of stuck waiting for a bus that may never come.

"Hello."

"Hello, son."

I didn't sit on the rock, as I didn't want to delay what might happen that evening for fear I would become exhausted and faint again, as the nights had tended to do that.

"I'm going to go across the street," I said as I set off.

The man in the hat didn't reply, but when I looked back, I saw him watching me crossing the street. I got to the other side and leaned against the lamppost. The man in the hat was looking straight at me, which was odd because he would usually face the ravine or down the street. It was uncomfortable being stared at by him, so I turned my eyes down at the pavement and then back towards the bushes.

"Young man."

"Yes. I'm here," I replied with excitement.

"Come. Come into the bushes. I want to show you something."

I pushed through the bushes like I did the night before. Once I felt no more scratching, I saw the desert-like surrounding that I'd seen the previous night. I again felt the rich air and took in the yellow-orange glow of the 360-degree-horizon.

The anticipation of the previous night crept up on me with perspiration gathering under my arms and warmth in my chest. I sat in the center once again without being directed by the voice.

"Take a deep breath," the voice instructed.

I did and closed my eyes as I did previously.

I waited for some time and once again became impatient, so I opened them and saw the entity in front of me. It was the same entity as the previous night, but its movement was different. Its colors weren't as bright. Not knowing what I should do, I closed my eyes, not because it was difficult to follow, but because I was simply hoping to revisit what I experienced.

I waited for the sensation to run through my fingertips, but that didn't happen. Something was different that night. I did start to feel something, but it wasn't in my fingertips. This time it was in my chest. I saw the image of a blank face say something to me. The pain tightened as if a little stone was stuck in my chest. I didn't care for it at all. My immediate reaction to the pressure was to place my hand over my chest, at which point I opened my eyes and stood up gasping for breath.

The blank face was gone, but inexplicably, I knew who it was. The entity changed to a gritty sand-like texture as it hovered in front of me. Suddenly, it turned into particles of sand and then blew off and fell into the desert-like surface and blended into the hundreds of millions of particles beneath my shoes.

It's gone!

She's gone!

The young woman in brown hair from the last night and the night before . . . *gone!*

I knelt in front of the general area where the sand from the entity dispersed and pushed my hands through the granules in a desperate attempt to find it. I leaned back while still on my knees. I couldn't see or hear anything. The last night and the sweetness of the night before were just memories. Fear came over me. *What if that is it? No more. No more warming of my heart. No more sensual pleasures. The woman with the brown hair and brown eyes may never be back!*

I straightened my legs and sat with them stretched out, looking at the horizon, the yellow-orange glow in the distance. I felt too weak to get up, and the tightness in my chest didn't go away. My panic and disbelief changed to emptiness and loneliness. I had no energy to move or think of what I would do next. I called out to the voice.

"Hello?"

Nothing.

As I sat, I became cold and clammy. I brought my legs in closer and wrapped them with my arms, rocking to keep warm. This rush of energy came up from my chest to where the tightness was, and tears filled my eyes. I pushed it down as best I could, but the teardrops grew larger and rolled down my cheeks. My chin and lower lip quivered. I pushed the tears off my face in embarrassment as if someone were watching me. I lowered my head between my knees and covered my face with my hands as I cried. The tightness in my chest began to release, so I just let it go. I opened my eyes and saw my teardrops fall into the sand as they rolled off my cheeks. I raised my head, sat for a moment, and scanned the horizon, unsure of what to do. I took several deep breaths until the tears stopped.

How am I going to get out of here?

I stood and did another 360-degree viewing. It was the same horizon wherever I looked. I started in one direction away from the center. I strode and saw nothing but the starkness of the desert. There was no odor, no wind or breeze, no noise in the distance, just the sound of my footsteps and my breathing. I felt far away from anything and anyone, but I kept going.

The image of the young woman with brown hair became suddenly clearer. I recalled the image of her face and the tone of her voice when she spoke, and then I remembered the tender touch of her energy. It made me feel good and strong again even knowing she was gone. I thought of the man in the hat. *Why does he not know where he's going? Something must be stopping him.*

I covered what seemed miles and miles, and I could see the horizon ahead of me becoming brighter, which gave me hope and energy. It dimmed behind me, however. *Something must be this way. Keep going.*

After what seemed hours, time felt as if it were standing still. Aiming towards the bright orange horizon, I became warmer. Ahead I could see something peaking on the horizon. In excitement, my pace picked up, and the crunch of my footsteps on the firm desert sand became louder. The image was clear now: it appeared to be a tower with a large stick-like figure on top with two wooden arm-like pieces dangling from it. The structure was made of stone and had a large wooden door with an iron handle. I approached the door, grabbed the handle, pulled the heavy door open, and peeked inside. The door creaked as it opened, but I thought that was all it would do until I put my full body into it to open it all the way.

"Hello!" I shouted.

Once I entered, I immediately noticed an old workbench supporting a telescope and an odd-looking machine. As I approached the instrument, I determined that it was turned on, which caused me to continue searching.

"Hello!" I shouted a little more loudly, but no answer.

Behind the bench was another door. I opened it slowly and could hear the squeaky wheels of a pulley wheel and line, much like a clothesline. The pulley system had pieces of paper attached, moving upwards but nothing returning on the way down. The line came from a larger hole in the floor of the tower, but there was nowhere to enter.

A ladder beside the conveyor headed to the top, where there was an opening. I decided to climb it. Once I reached the top of the tower, the line of the pulley transferred to another pulley wheel, which transported the paper far out to what looked like a telephone pole and onto another telephone pole and so on until it escaped my field of vision. I climbed back down and entered the main room to grab the telescope and returned. I cleaned the lens with my shirt and focused on the line. The poles led to another tower far off in the distance about five or so miles away. With the telescope, I could also see that the orange glow was more of a ball of heat with smoke rising high above.

The brightness of the ball hurt my eyes. I winced, and I looked back down at the squeaky pulley system and tried to have a better view of what it was carrying. The pieces of paper had some type of writing on them. Each had a different style of printed writing: handwriting, typed writing, some in English and some in other languages. Some of these pieces of paper had names on the outside. "Gary," "Charles," "Anthony," "Elizabeth" and many others that I couldn't understand. Trying to follow these names blurred my vision, so I had to stop. These were notes or messages of some kind, but I dared not touch them.

I took the telescope and climbed back down the ladder. The machine was still humming as I exited past the big heavy door. It took much effort to close it.

I followed the poles with the intent of reaching the other tower. The firm desert began to change to looser sand, which felt dry and became difficult to walk in. Every once in a while, I took out the telescope to check how far I was from the second tower. In the view of the telescope, midway between the second tower, I noticed a clump of large rocks buried in the sand. After another mile, I discovered that one of the large rocks had been cut to give the image of two eyes and a nose.

Once I covered a few more miles, the image of the tower became clearer, and the orange glow was greater. The second tower closely resembled the first in that it was also made of stone and had a large door and the same stick configuration on top that appeared to be inoperable. Before I entered, I followed the wire from the first tower. It continued over top of the second tower and onwards, but I couldn't determine to where. I noticed another clump of large stones just outside the second tower. Upon approaching it, I determined that one of the large stones had an eye and a nose similar to the first, but this one wasn't buried as much and indeed had two eyes. I knelt and brushed some sand off of the face of the stone to study the detail. *This must be a statue of some sort that had fallen.* I peered up. The orange glow was very strong, and I got a better view of the smoke escaping from its glow, but I wanted an even better view, so I entered the second tower.

I could hear faint voices coming from inside. I couldn't make out what they were saying. I entered, to hear a static and faint voice of a young child.

"Mommy. This is Freddy. When will I see you again, Mommy? Mommy, this is Freddy. When will I see you again? Mommy, this is Freddy. When do I get to see you again, Mommy?"

In front was a bench with a speaker box from where the child's voice was emanating. A microphone was situated beside it. The voice stopped, followed by a low hum. Beside the speaker box were rubber stamps, an ink pen, a piece of paper, and a dried-up ink jar. The desk had little pockets to place notes or envelopes. As I stepped closer to the bench, the beginning of an unfinished letter read:

> "Dear Mother,
>
> I hope you and father are well. Please don't worry about me and the boys. My mates are like brothers to me. Please tell father . . ."

I continued scanning the room to spy a candle and an oil lamp on a shelf. I opened the door beside the desk. There were no pulleys, but a ladder to the top, which I ascended. Once on top, I was enthralled by a skeleton of a large bird and the awkwardly positioned wooden arms of the tall structure. I took out the telescope to gain a full view of the orange glow from that vantage point. The glow was a great ball of flames. It was so bright, it stung to continue and turned to the line instead. The squeaky pulley wheels kept moving, sending the little messages from where I was to another tower towards the glow. This tower's wooden arms moved. One of the two arms would be up and the other down, and then moved again.

"There must be someone there!" I said aloud.

More clumps of rock. More and more clumps showed up as I viewed the landscape between the two towers. I put the telescope away in my jacket and made my way back down the ladder and out of the first door. More voices came from the speaker box on the bench. "Hello, Charlie. Your sister will be visiting us from . . ." And then became static and muffled and couldn't hear the rest of the message. "The train will arrive . . ." muffled again so I left through the large door.

The closer I became; the orange glow turned to a ball of fire. I needed to see who was in the 3rd tower. *Maybe they can tell me how to get out of here.* Homesick and lonely, I felt far away, and the love that the voice introduced me to seemed so distant that I could barely remember the experience. Perhaps it was because I was so preoccupied with finding my way back.

I approached another clump. These rocks were the same size and looked as if they were of the same style as in the statue I came across earlier. This one had two eyes and a nose and no mouth. I did not stop as I wanted to get to the third tower quickly. I placed my hand over my forehead to block the brightness of the fireball. I was becoming exhausted with the amount of effort from the dry sand and the heat from the fire. I kept going for another five miles or so.

The tower was in sight, but the arms on top had stopped moving. The door was left open. When I arrived at the base of the tower with the bright orange glow behind it, I determined that the tower was situated on a cliff. Peering down at it, I spied two more clumps of rocks. The wire with messages on it went from the top of the third tower and continued towards the fireball. I turned around and peeked through the slightly opened door.

"Hello!"

Nothing.

There was another bench with another odd-looking machine, which was also humming. It gave off static noise, but nothing came out. I stepped around the desk to the tower. It was also left open, so I climbed it, but no one was there.

"Where did he go?" I was disappointed.

I removed the telescope, which showed me that the wire with the paper made its way right into the fireball. *What was the point of all these messages being burnt?* I continued to scan around it as best I could when I saw a very large man and then another, and then another. They were tending to the fire.

I knelt for fear of being spotted.

I turned my back against the side of the tower wall and rested for a moment. I closed my eyes and could feel myself drift off, so I opened them quickly and slapped my face. I couldn't afford to fall asleep. I needed to get home. I placed the telescope onto the base of the wooden-armed structure, got back to my knees, and scanned the surroundings. There were two clumps of bushes and a small grouping of trees in the distance. Between the tower and the clumps of bushes were footprints.

"There! That's where he went!"

I hurried down the ladder and out the two doors to follow the steps in the sand. I was worn out and needed to sleep but I couldn't stop. *I need to get home.*

"Hello," I said as I approached the trees. "Can you help me? I need to get home."

I entered the treed area which was now cool and dark.

"Hello? Please?" I yelled in desperation. "Help?"

The trees became dense, but I kept on pushing until I saw it break through and the light above opened up. I pushed through more of the bushes until I was on the sidewalk in front of the lamppost. I leaned over, trying to catch my breath. I stood. The man in the hat was still waiting.

I paused for a moment. I crossed the street and sat on the rock.

"Did you have an interesting journey?" the man asked.

"I certainly did!"

I sat thinking of all that happened since I entered the bush that night. It seemed as if I had been gone for days, but while sitting on that rock, I determined I hadn't. Time seemed completely irrelevant. I put my face in my hands and took deep breaths. I started to go over everything in my head as to what happened. The details were not clear. I started to feel dizzy as I wasn't thinking very linearly.

"I'm not feeling well, sir. I will see you tomorrow," I said, almost sick to my stomach.

I got up and started towards the house.

Saturday, May 5, 1984, 3:19 a.m.

Sitting on the rock near the man in the hat, I still felt drained from the previous night. *What is he going to do? Will he ever board that bus? What is stopping him? It's wearing me out. I'm weaker and weaker night by night, but something is drawing me to come from my house to see him. I'm restless. I can't sit here any longer. I need to see if the voice is still there. I need answers.* I pushed myself off the rock and headed towards the other side of the street quite briskly this time. I made my way to the lamp post and waited for the voice.

"Welcome back," the voice said. "You had quite the adventure last night, didn't you?"

"You abandoned me!" I said firmly in disappointment.

"Not at all. I was with you the entire time, but some things you need to experience on your own. You did very well. You should be proud of yourself."

"What happened to the young lady with the brown hair?" I asked as a lump formed in my throat.

"You must understand, that to be alive, one must feel all, and until last night, you had not."

Before I could reply, the voice continued.

"Tonight, however; will not be about you."

"Oh?"

"Your friend across the street. He needs your help."

"Yes, I know. He's stuck."

"Yes. He needs your help, and I'm going to give you guidance."

"I want to help."

"You have a good heart, young man; now come into the bushes."

I did.

I made my way through the bushes and arrived at a familiar place; the center. As I sat and closed my eyes, I anticipated further direction from the voice. I waited with my eyes closed once again but no response. When I re-opened them, I recognized the same horizon from the previous night, so I started in a direction from the center towards the horizon.

I stopped and thought: *I have no idea what direction I went last night. The towers were miles away, therefore I couldn't possibly see them from here. How am I to help the man in the hat? I don't even know who he is. Does he even have a name? Silly me didn't even ask him.*

The ground was firm and could hear nothing but my footsteps and the sound of my breathing. Bits and pieces of last night came back to me. The sand becoming dryer. The giant ball of fire. The entity and how it left me feeling empty before it disappeared. The love and affection and passion from the previous nights. I had to admit, despite the way it ended, those were memories I still enjoyed. I remembered the pulley wheels and the wire; the fallen statues and how they formed clumps of large rock.

As I continued, it occurred to me that the orange glow before me was growing, which told me I was going back in the direction I had last night and therefore should see the first tower before long. Something caused me to stop and whirl around.

A shadow!

I don't recall seeing my shadow last night. That's disconcerting. I guess I didn't notice. Once in a while, I would turn back and study my shadow as I traveled on. It was the image of my body stretched over the firm desert floor, my arms swinging back and forth.

"Hello!" I said to my shadow.

I turned forward and continued towards the orange glow.

Mile after mile towards the orange glow. The heat became warmer again and the firm earth slowly changed to loose sand once again, however; the landscape was different than I remembered the previous night. In the distance, I could see a hill and the faint image of an even larger hill farther ahead of it. And the ripple of the sand as if it had been blown by a wind, even though there was none that night. Beyond the hill, I saw a clump of large rocks similar to the ones the previous night. This one had the same facial features.

Why were all these statues fallen? I crouched. Yes, two eyes, a nose, and no mouth. My shadow crouched too. I stood and watched my shadow stand. *This is not the same way I went last night as I would have seen the first tower by now.* I passed the small hill, heading towards a larger hill, where the glow peeked out from behind it.

I felt scorched by the heat of the giant fireball. I was closer than I thought! I must have come from a different direction, as I would have seen the third tower by that point.

I placed my hands over my forehead. I saw faint objects walking around the fire, but I couldn't quite make out what or who they were. Maybe it was the same large men as from the previous night. There was a cliff in the far distance on the other side of the fireball, but no tower.

Once I got to the larger hill, there appeared a cave with a large entrance. It was hot, and I was tired so started towards the entrance but stopped. I was nervous about entering. I studied my shadow and wondered what I was going to do, as I had no way of knowing how to help the man in the hat, and I was lost. There were no towers in sight, but I was close to the giant fireball. I stood still. My shadow moved slightly to the left and then to the right.

I turned around quickly for fear that there was someone behind me, but there wasn't.

I turned back around, and my shadow pointed with one arm toward the cave. I had no arms raised.

Seeing the dark cave entrance, I was reluctant, but I had to go in. *Maybe my answer for the man in the hat is in this cave.* I headed slowly toward the entrance, as the heat from the fireball fell behind the hill. As I stepped into the cave, I could only see darkness, but the coolness of the cave was a relief. I hesitantly continued into the cool moist air; water dripped from its ceiling. I listened to the running of water farther down the cave.

"Hello!" I called.

The echo scared me, as it was louder than I thought it would be. No one answered. The cave was very high. As I rounded the corner, I came upon two larger rocks blocking my way. Once my eyes adjusted, I discovered that it was the same type of rock that I encountered earlier in the clumps. The face was the same. Two closed eyes a nose and no mouth. The head was a rock on top of another larger rock a torso. There were two arms, forearms, and hands. The legs were the large stones blocking my way as it sat in the cave. It was cool and damp, with moss growing around it. It appeared to have been there for some time.

I climbed on top of one of the rock legs and stepped in closer: there was something placed between the two hands of the large stone man - a glass jar with a folded note inside. *Could this be the help that the man in the hat needs? I need to get this message to him in the hat and the only way I know back to him is in the bushes near the third tower. I must find that third tower!* I traced the image in front of me from its head to its legs and feet, wondering why it was there and why it had that jar with a note stuck in it. *I must take the jar.*

Being careful not to smash the glass, I slid the jar out of the stone hands of the sculpture. As soon as the glass jar was out, I heard a low rumbling sound much like thunder. I made my way out of the cave in view of the fireball. Nothing was behind me, not even my shadow. I placed my hand over my eyes to block the bright light. Around the orange fireball, I did see something.

Dust kicked up around the fire like a windstorm.

I hiked towards where the tower should have been, as I needed to get back to the man in the hat.

I stopped and brought my hand back up to my forehead to look. It wasn't a windstorm, but three large men were now headed in my direction.

I walked faster as I needed to reach the tower before they came, but it was nowhere in sight!

I ran, but the quicker I went, the closer the large men were. It now appeared to me that these men were not large men at all! These were giant rock men. They had to be thirty feet tall! These stone men rushed towards me so I turned and headed for the cave.

The ground shook. Because of their giant stretch, they were gaining on me. I wasn't sure if I was going to make it back to the cave. I heard a loud crash: one of the three men fell into a pile in the sand as the other two kept running after me. I was frightened beyond belief, as these giant stone men would likely crush me. I heard another loud crash and turned to see the second large stone man fall to a heap of rocks, but the last one kept running after me.

I made it into the cave. Once in, I worried that the other large man inside would come alive, but he was still sitting there. The last giant stopped in front of the cave opening. I waited to see if he was going to try and come in or was going to carry on, but before

I could think my next step through, the large stone man fell into a pile of rocks in front of the entrance.

I waited to see if anything else was running after me but heard nothing. My legs gave way under me and I fell to the floor, nearly paralyzed. I held the jar tight in my arm while looking at the cave entrance to see if I could make it back out or not. I sat there for a moment to catch my breath. I eventually stood and tentatively made my way towards the pile of rocks that were once a giant man. They didn't move. The face of the rock was emotionless, like they all were, dead or alive. I stretched my hand toward the large stones, which gave off much heat. I examined the pile and determined I could make my way out by climbing over them, which I did.

There appeared to be no dust storms or large stone men in or around the ball of fire.

For what seemed hours, I made my way around the perimeter of the giant orange fireball with hopes of seeing the third tower on the cliff, but I began to wonder if I had imagined it, as I was on the cliff and saw no tower or treed area. I eventually returned to the cave to gain relief from the heat.

I climbed back over the collapsed giant and into the cave and sat on the damp ground, leaning up against the wall beside the stone man that had the jar. I held the jar up to the little bit of sunlight that shone through the cave entrance. *This note must be of some significance for the stone man to be holding this and the others to chase me for it. How am I going to get this to the man in the hat? How am I going to get home?*

I sat in the cave wondering how long I'd been away. The coolness and moisture of the air in the cave were relaxing and soothing. *I need to get this to the man in the hat before I fall back asleep.* As I sat, I wondered what the message was. *Was it from a lover or maybe from a loved one, a close family member maybe?* It was not my message, and I certainly wasn't going to read it.

There was a rushy sound coming from the other end of the cave. I was getting drowsy, so I got back up and climbed over the large stone man's legs and farther down the cave. As I explored further, the opening became narrower to the point where I had to duck my head.

The cave walls and floor were wet. The rest of which became a tunnel with a dim light at the other end. As I continued, I could hear the sound of water running at the other end of the tunnel. I poked my head out: a ravine with a stream burbled through it. In excitement, I ran through the stream to the other side, where the bushes were, in hopes of finding the street and presenting the man in the hat with the message in the jar. I pressed into the bushes aggressively, pushing forward, scratching my hands and face. I kept going forward -- but no sidewalk or streetlamp. I turned back into the ravine, took a few more breaths, and tried a different location. Again. I pushed through with one hand on the jar and the other covering my face but to no avail.

I came back out of the bush.

"Dammit!" I took a breath. "I'm lost," I said, hopeless and almost in tears.

When I got to the stream I sat on a fallen tree and held the jar in my hands, wondering what to do next. I needed to get this message to the man in the hat. I don't know what to do. *Should I go back in the tunnel?* I raised my head and didn't see the opening of the tunnel anymore. It disappeared.

"Young man?" the voice said in a questioning tone.

"Yes."

"You must understand, you can't take items out of the ravine. They must stay here."

I thought for a moment. "I don't understand."

"That jar . . ." the voice said firmly. "And the message in it. You cannot take it beyond the ravine. It is forbidden. That is why you had so much trouble with your stone friends earlier."

"This is for that man. He is standing there waiting and waiting." My eyes filled with tears, and my chin quivered.

"All is not lost."

"I don't know what you mean." I sobbed, wiping the tears away with my free hand as the other held the jar.

"You can still deliver the message."

"How?"

The voice didn't respond.

"I have to read it. Don't I?"

"Yes. Read it very carefully, then you shall put the message back in the jar and place it into the stream."

I placed my left hand over the lid and unscrewed the top. An unfamiliar odor came from it. It wasn't unpleasant, just an unrecognizable one. I took out the note and placed the jar and lid in front of me. I unfolded the typed note. It read:

```
              Please understand.

Just because I cannot be with you, does not
        mean that I do not love you.
```

I studied it to make sure I remembered the exact wording. I then folded the note, placed it in the jar, and closed the lid. I closed my eyes to memorize the words, then opened them and strode towards the stream. I crouched, placed the jar on the flowing water, and watched it go down the stream until it disappeared.

I made my way quite easily onto the sidewalk below the lamppost. The man in the hat across from me looked my way. I thought about the message again and worried that it might upset him. I made my way across the street and sat on the rock and looked across to the ravine. The stream of water gurgled behind the bushes.

"I have a message for you," I said to the man in the hat.

"You do?" he asked with surprise and turned his head towards me.

"Yes," I told him exactly what the message said.

The man turned his head back towards the street and stood quietly for a moment before his shoulders dropped a little and turned to me.

"May I sit down for a moment, son?" he asked politely.

"Of course!" I eagerly made way for him.

The man put down his suitcase, sat on the rock, and sighed with relief as one would after standing for so long. I moved back to give him space but couldn't see any emotion on his face, as it was covered by the brim of his hat. He did not seem upset. He leaned forward and placed his hands together as if he was thinking. I studied his hands as he did this: they were of an elderly man. He was thinking about the message he received, so I gave him some space.

"Thank you."

"You're welcome."

Something changed in him. Not only was the tone of his voice more relaxed and casual, but even his body language was more human, versus the stiff man I'd seen night after night.

A sound emanated from down the street -- the bus again. The man in the hat grabbed his suitcase, rose quickly and when he was at the side of the street, the bus stopped in front of him, opening the doors. He turned and waved to me, then boarded the bus, while removing his hat, showing his white thin hair. I could see his silhouette as he walked to the middle of the bus and took his seat, at which time the bus closed the doors, released its breaks, and made its way up the street until it was out of sight.

I returned to the rock and sat. I looked up to the ravine, the bushes in front of it, and the light on the sidewalk from the lamppost. I sighed as I did. I took in the night air. I pondered going back across the road, but my body was telling me it was time to go.

What a lovely night this had been.

Part 2

The Red Balloon

Saturday, June 2, 1984, 3:02 am

Tick, tick, tick, tick . . . I heard, as I slowly opened my eyes to see the darkness in my room.

Uh oh! It's happening again. I'm waking up in the middle of the night. I hope this is just a one-night thing. I turned on my lamp and searched for the clock. Yup. Just after three in the morning. I looked at the ceiling to see the streetlights poking through the top of the drapes. It had been almost a month since my last bout of sleepless nights. I lay there waiting and waiting to feel tired.

I took my feet from underneath my covers, pushed myself off the bed, and made my way to the window, where I opened the drapes. I let the drape close, and just as I was about to step away from the window, I stopped. What was that red thing I just saw? I pulled the drape open. There was a red balloon hovering beside the rock. Something dangled from its string. *This . . . I must look into.*

The night air was still cool, so off I went with my jacket and carried my shoes in hand until I left the house. I put them on, rounded the corner, and headed down the hill toward the rock. Even though there was no one there, I still strolled casually, leisurely, towards the balloon. It was quite an eerie feeling with it just hanging there as if an invisible person were holding the string, which is why I approached it slowly. I didn't grab the string or touch the balloon but instead circled it.

I sat on the rock and observed it. There was a letter of some sort wrapped up in a little bundle at the end of the string. It dangled and twirled as I watched. Curiosity got the better of me, so I got up from the rock and unraveled the package.

The letter read:

```
Help me, please. I am lost!

Will you help me?

If so, please take this letter
and keep it in a very safe
place.

If you do not wish to help me,
please re-attach it and I will
be on my way to search for help
elsewhere.
```

How am I supposed to help a silly red balloon in the middle of the night?

I returned to the rock and watched the balloon hover in front of me for a moment. It rose up and up above the trees of the ravine and over until I couldn't see it anymore.

I folded the letter and stuck it into the right pocket of my pants.

Sunday, June 3, 1984, 3:14 am

I woke up to the sound of a clicking noise on my window. As I opened the drapes, I realized nothing unusual was outside. I did however see the red balloon as it was last night, hovering beside the rock with another package dangling from it.

I went down the hill, letting the night air enter my lungs. It was uplifting, clear, and pure. Once at the rock, I sat on it and released the package tied to the string to unravel it. It was another letter. It read:

> Please take the letter you received from me yesterday and re-attach it to the balloon.
>
> Keep this letter that you are reading now in a safe place. Bring it with you tomorrow, as it will prove helpful.

I reached for the letter inside my right pant pocket, but before I reattached it, I attempted to read it again. The letter was different from the previous night. It had markings that I couldn't make out. It wasn't like the letters became smudged, but it was a deliberate type of characters. I hesitated for a moment, thinking back to the previous night, as I was certain that the red balloon was asking for help. I folded the letter together tightly, wrapped the string I had from that day's message tightly, and re-attached it to the balloon.

I placed the letter into my jacket pocket. I sat on the rock and watched the balloon as it bounced in midair. The balloon rose until it was over the trees and out of sight.

I re-read it to make sure I wasn't imagining anything.

```
Please take the letter you
received from me yesterday and
re-attach it to the balloon.

Keep this letter that you are
reading now in a safe place.
Bring it with you tomorrow as
it will prove helpful.
```

I sat there wondering what this was all about.

Monday, June 4, 1984, 3:09 am

I woke up to the sound of a clicking noise on my window again. As I opened the drapes, I peered out with the expectation of seeing the familiar red balloon, but I did not. I closed and opened my eyes a few times to let the water moisten them so my vision would be clearer. Still no red balloon. I reached for my jacket and searched the right pocket for the letter from the previous night and opened it.

To my surprise, I couldn't read it. The writing turned into the same symbol-like characters in the previous night's letter. *I don't understand.* I started to feel bad, thinking that I may not have left the letter in a safe enough place. Maybe the balloon hadn't arrived yet, so I grabbed my shoes and jacket and made my way down to the rock.

Once by the side of the street, I sat and waited for the red balloon. The night air was very still. It was cool in the evening for June. I looked up over the tops of the trees of the ravine in case I could see the balloon coming over. Nothing.

I heard a mysterious distant sound come from the north side of the street. It was a dog trotting towards me with its nails clicking on the pavement. A Golden Retriever with a red paisley-styled bandana wrapped around its neck.

"Well, hello," I said as it came towards me and sat. "Are you lost?" I rubbed its head and behind its ears as it panted. It was a larger male with orange-blond hair and a very soft coat. I checked to see if there was a name tag -- but no name. I had to call him something.

"Here, boy. Why are you out so late? Couldn't sleep either? Your owner must be worried."

I hoped there was someone down the street, but it was empty.

He had enough of my petting, and he headed back down the street again, so I remained where I was, as I was sure he knew his way home. The dog then crossed the street towards the ravine and stopped just outside the treed area where a pathway began. The dog sat and turned his head towards me.

Strange. I don't recall seeing a pathway there before, but why is the dog just sitting there? He didn't come from that direction.

The dog whined, circled and sat down in the same spot, and stared at me. *He must be telling me something.* I made my way toward the pathway. Just as I got closer to him, he took off towards the ravine.

"Here, boy!" I yelled after he was out of sight, but he didn't return.

I headed towards the pathway entrance and stopped. There he was, his body pointed towards the pathway, but his head turned towards me. He then bolted ahead. He was leading me somewhere.

I went along the twisty-turny narrow dirt pathway with the tree branches brushing against my jacket. I got this eerie feeling something was going to jump out at me. The trees and bushes became quite dense, and the pathway narrowed. Once in a while, I would lose sight of the dog as he was going faster than I was. He would stop and look back.

Eventually, he led me to a clearing just large enough to make way for a bench. Beside the bench, the red balloon hovered with another package dangling from it. I took a seat and removed the package while the dog sat beside my feet. The balloon rose into the air and eventually over the trees and out of sight again.

The dog watched the direction where the balloon had disappeared to.

The package was heavier than the previous night. I unraveled it, and out came a pair of eyeglasses -- no letter, just a pair of glasses. I studied them for a moment, curious as to why the red balloon would contain such an item. They were a simple thin steel black frame pair with the arms folded. Not sure what to do with them, I opened the arms and lifted them into the sky to check the lenses.

"Well, boy. Maybe I'd better try these on."

As soon as I placed them on, the entire scenery changed. The pathway remained, but the trees disappeared, and I could only see a long green meadow scene with rolling hills in the hazy distance. The sky was a solid color of bright blue as If I were in a movie set. It was almost bright enough to be daylight. Amazed at what I was seeing, I blinked a few times to make sure I wasn't imagining things, and then I removed them.

The scenery was back to how it was when I arrived in the clearing.

"Wow!"

The dog raised his head and turned it slightly as if to ask a question.

"It's OK, boy." I patted his head while he wagged his tail.

I put the glasses back on and stood to scan the scenery. Behind me, I just could make out a long pathway that led over a large hill, I couldn't see beyond it. In front of me, the path curved over a hill and disappeared.

I leaned down to pat the dog, but he had gone.

"Here, boy!"

I heard his bark from beyond the hill ahead, so I followed the sound.

"Here, boy!" The dog barked again in the distance, so I picked up the pace.

I climbed the hill where I stopped to take in the view. In front of me, the path widened and then branched off into three smaller paths. From where the paths split away, I could see the meadow was not long grass, but many pods floating on tiny little pedestal-like plants.

Some of the pods were clear with a center that swirled around as the pod moved ever-so-slightly. Some of the pods were frosted over containing a fluffy white substance. Some of the pedestals were empty. Some of the pods lowered from the sky and landed perfectly on an empty pedestal.

"What are these?" I asked myself.

I made my way down the middle path and knelt. I touched one of the frosted white pods with my forefinger. I felt a rush of energy run from my fingertip and through my body, but it also created the flash of an image in my mind. I withdrew my hand as my first reaction was fear.

"What was that?" I jumped up.

I thought about what just happened. It wasn't bad. It didn't feel bad at all. It gave me some type of emotional warmth. The image was difficult to describe, but if I had to re-tell it, it was of a middle-aged man, welcoming me. Welcoming me to what? I don't know.

I knelt and touched the pod again. This time I closed my eyes to get a better image. The energy ran through me like before. The warmth was similar to spending time with an old family member whom I always enjoyed. The picture was clearer at that point. The man had eyeglasses. He was saying something.

He wasn't speaking to me specifically, but I was there, in a room. In the middle of the room were three large tables placed end to end to form a large makeshift table. Around them were a goodly number of chairs, plates, and cutlery for dinner. The middle-aged man hugged and greeted many, many guests. I watched as they all lined up to greet the man in the glasses. I could tell that every one of his guests was delighted by him. I felt as if I knew the man.

I released my finger from the pod and the warmth went away.

I stood and viewed the other pods. All of these had the same frosted covering.

I left that path and took another from where the main one branched off. These were clear pods. I knelt again, touched one, and closed my eyes. A different sort of energy came over me. The feeling of confusion and anxiety, then a calmness. A vision of an elderly woman appeared. She was talking to me. The specific directions she gave me weren't exactly clear, but her reasoning made sense, and that's what made my earlier anxiety fade. She touched my cheeks with both of her hands. Again, I felt like I knew this woman somehow.

I released my fingers from the pod and stood there taking in the rows and hills of pods. Each of the three pathways branched off to another three paths until I couldn't see any farther.

"Here, boy," I called.

I heard barking coming from where the third path led.

I traveled along it to find him, as he had a habit of running off on me. As I carried on along it, it became clear that these pedestals were empty: no pods. The dog barked farther up from the path which had twisted in between two hills. I still couldn't see him.

Beyond the two hills, the path ended at a very small building that had no windows. I could hear the clinking of dishes and glass from beyond. *Maybe this is a restaurant of some sort; an odd place for it.* I gave the door a knock.

No one came to answer, so I hesitantly opened it to see a dimly lit pub. In the center was a square-shaped bar with a stern-looking man leaning against it. Several stools were placed around it, and beyond the square were several small tables with chairs.

I entered and sat on one end. The bartender had a full beard and nicely combed black hair and wore a striped vest and a white puffy shirt underneath it. Shortly after I took my seat, he approached me from inside the bar, opened his arms, and placed them on either side as if to hold himself up, a rather intimidating stance.

"What are you having?"

"Ummmm." My voice trembled a little. "I'll have a beer, please."

He grabbed a glass from the counter, tipped it under the spout, and drew the beer. He placed the glass on the counter in front of me and went on with his tidying up. I sipped my cold beverage and checked out the place. There were four people: a woman who was sitting at a table with someone, an unshaven man in the corner beside the entrance, and a man with glasses, sitting at the bar across from me. He kept staring at me through the rectangular frames.

I turned away from the man staring and perused the room. There was only a little bit of light peeking through the closed shutters. The place was low-key except for the clanking of the glasses and the woman talking with someone. There was a heaviness in the air with the smell of stale beer. My eyes met with the bartenders. He stared at me as if I wasn't to be trusted.

I wondered: *How am I going to pay for this beer?* Panicking, I reached into my jacket pocket for my wallet, but all I could find was the letter from the red balloon, which I had forgotten about. I decided to open it. To my surprise, I could make out what it said, but it was different from the previous night.

> Please read this carefully --
> you will not be able to hold on
> to this letter long, as you
> will eventually find out.
>
> At some point during this
> journey, you will find yourself
> inside a pub. You will discover
> me there.

When I raised my eyes from my letter, the bartender glared at me sternly as if he'd caught me in some illegal act. He lifted his left hand, reached it towards me, and motioned with his fingers to hand over the letter. I hesitated for a moment, then calmly folded it and gave it to the bartender. He poured a shot of whiskey and slapped it on the counter in front of me.

"Is this for me?" I asked, surprised.

The bartender pointed towards the table where the woman was sitting. Her back was towards me. I turned back to the bartender who slid the shot of whiskey in front.

The woman got up from her chair and sauntered towards me. She came very close, stretching out her neck a little. She had long black straight hair. I don't know exactly why, but I was immediately attracted to her. She continued studying me before forming a smile. Forgetting I had glasses on, I lifted my right hand to remove them when she reached for my hand to stop.

"No. Don't. I like them on you," she said, as her hand pleasantly pushed mine down to the bar.

My attraction grew. Her head slightly tilted and her brown eyes studied me, almost piercing mine. I felt as if I knew her from somewhere and the familiarity made me more attracted. She stood for a moment, silent, but still gazing, creating a bit of awkwardness.

"You came here looking for me, didn't you?" she asked.

"I'm not sure . . ." I replied, "but I am looking for someone."

"Oh? And who might that be?" she asked, with her head tilted even more.

"I don't quite know yet. I'll know when I find him . . . or her?"

"Hmmm." She responded with a tone of disappointment. "So . . . you don't want me?"

"No. I didn't say that at all."

The woman turned her head toward the person she was sitting with. Her body was blocking, so I couldn't see what expression was on the person's face. When she turned back, her face changed. Her eyebrows raised with sadness.

"I didn't mean it that--" I began to say but was cut off.

"By the way. Why are you here?" she asked, studying me again. "You don't belong here, do you? You don't like me . . . do you?"

"Why would you say such a thing? I don't even know you."

"You don't know me?" she repeated in a sarcastic tone, letting out a devilish grin. "Oh yes, you do. More than you think. Drink your whiskey. I got it for you."

She turned her back on me, walked towards the table, and re-took her seat.

I know her from somewhere. But from where?

I took the shot glass and downed the whiskey. As I put it down, the sudden burn down my throat made me cough and my eyes water. The effect of the whiskey suddenly made me very relaxed. I almost felt as if I could fall asleep right there and then. I shut my eyes for just a few seconds and then it hit me!

The image of that woman entered my mind as if she was in my dream, but I wasn't sleeping. I opened my eyes and I was back in the pub. She must have entered one of my dreams.

While the alcohol was still burning my stomach, I closed my eyes once again to see her in that dreamy state. It was quite mystical and wonderful with the sense of kinship and the coziness that came into my chest when I saw her with my eyes closed. It was the same feeling I get when I wake up in the morning from a good dream and I'm reminded of it in the middle of the waking day.

The image of her faded as the alcohol stopped burning. I opened my eyes. I wanted to go up to her and tell her how I just felt, but I hesitated. *Maybe it's not the most appropriate time.* She was with someone anyway.

Across the bar, the man with the rectangular glasses still stared at me as he was before. I turned to see the bartender leaning against the inside of the bar, with his arms crossed. The unshaven man in the corner was also regarding me. I felt uncomfortable, so I took a few sips of my beer. I made every attempt to avoid eye contact with either of the three men, but I reminded myself that I need to find my lost friend. *Is it one of these people? Is it the woman I was just talking to?* I doubted how I could help this lost person. I took another sip of my beer and saw in the corner of my eye the unshaven man waving to me discreetly from the table.

I grabbed my beer, walked over to his table, and sat across from him. He leaned towards me.

"You're not supposed to be here!" he whispered.

"What do you mean?"

"Shhh! I don't want anyone to hear us," he urged, still leaning towards me. "You see. I want to leave, but I'm scared to death of it. I don't know what's out there, but that's not the only thing. I am afraid of them finding out I want to leave. You see..." he said, scanning the room back and forth before he spoke again. "They need me. I entertain them." He said a little more relaxed.

"How so?" I whispered.

"I tell them stories. They love them. My stories occupy their minds. But . . . I'm tired. I'm tired of telling tales," he said with a droop around his mouth. "I do have one I need to share with you. It's true. This one was told to me by my uncle Tom. He told me lots of them, but this one is important."

"Bartender!" The unshaven man called out. "Another whiskey for the young man."

Moments later the shot came, and I downed it.

The unshaven man recited this.

The missing letter of Geraldine Thompson

Geraldine Thompson was a respected citizen of the community. She came from a wealthy family and was well-educated. She married at the age of twenty-three but soon after divorced her husband with whom she had no children. Geraldine lived most of her life alone, writing the odd article for the local newspaper and attending a few local events. She never remarried, but she had three lovers in the span of several years between her late forties and early fifties. She continued to remain single afterward. While in her late sixties, Geraldine became unwell and died at the age of sixty-eight.

The rumor is that when Geraldine became aware of her illness, she decided to write each of her past three lovers a letter. The letters were simply to express her gratitude for what each brought to her life. There were very few people close to Geraldine. Her friend Mary was likely the only one close enough to share these memories with. Although some memories were painful, Geraldine did not regret having these men in her life and more importantly felt complete with life after she had written the letters to her past three lovers. She wrote each letter, knowing that each man was still alive and, with a little bit of help, was able to find where they had lived. Some men had married; some did not, but that didn't stop her from sending the letters.

Mary was beside Geraldine while she was very sick. While the two were alone, and although Geraldine was quite ill and tired, she had enough energy to tell her friend about her three lovers and their stories.

Lawrence

Oh, Lawrence! He was my protector, my guardian angel of sorts. He was my first lover after so many years of being alone. How I met him was quite a silly chain of events, which started with a simple leaky bathroom sink. While talking to Mrs. Roberts at the post office, I mentioned to her that I needed a plumber to fix my bathroom sink. The constant dripping drove me crazy! Mrs. Roberts recommended her nephew and so gave me his number. When Lawrence came to my door, I was quite surprised, as I was expecting a much younger man. Instead, he was middle-aged, like me.

Although he was very polite when he introduced himself, I was taken aback by his frame. He was a husky man with broad shoulders and large strong arms and hands. I led him upstairs to the bathroom where he examined the faucet and determined it to be a simple fix and continued to grab his tools. I went about my business and fixed a pot of tea for myself as it was the middle of the day and I needed a sandwich. As Lawrence continued up the stairs, I began to lose interest in the article I was reading and became more interested in how this man was making out with the leaky faucet. I heard some clunking and moving around, so I left the kitchen and poked my head around the corner, and strolled up to ask him if he needed me to move anything.

He replied with a pleasant "no thank you." I wandered back to the table to fix my tea and found myself walking back up the stairs to check on him again. Once in the bathroom, I could see this man lying with his back on the floor and face under the sink, and his large arms removing the faucet from below. I stood there for a moment quietly, not realizing it, but I was examining the man's frame and the movement of his arms as they worked. He couldn't see me, but rather than be discovered as if I was watching him or being nosey, I let my presence be known and asked if he would like a cup of tea.

Oh, poor Lawrence banged his head in surprise, which left a bloody gash on his forehead. I apologized and felt embarrassed. I ran down the hallway to grab a towel and placed it on his forehead to stop the bleeding. As I knelt with the towel pressed on his head, he lifted his hand and placed it over mine quite accidentally to hold the towel on. At that moment, I knew then I was attracted to the man.

He eventually fixed the sink and did join me for a cup of tea. We talked for some time. I discovered that he was divorced. I recall apologizing at least ten times, but he assured me it was just a scratch. I paid him for his work and told him I would call him again if I needed help.

As time went on, I found myself thinking of the moment he touched my hand. This just made my heart flutter. I gave it two weeks and finally came up with something that needed to be fixed. My back door never did shut quite right, and although I simply put up with it, I made it an excuse to call the man over.

He promptly replied and came over the following day. Lawrence easily fixed the door within five minutes. I had a pot of tea already simmering and he joined me and stayed for two hours as we talked and talked.

Lawrence came over quite often as he began to volunteer to repair minor things in my house and refused to take money. One time in the dead of night, there was a very loud thunderstorm. The wind was incredibly strong, and there came a loud banging coming from behind my house, which frightened me, as I was certain someone was trying to break in. I called Lawrence and he came right away.

He gave me a great big hug as he saw how terrified I was. His large physique holding me made me relieved and secure. He quickly went to the back of the house and discovered the garden shed door was flung open and had been swinging with the wind, creating that awful sound. He latched it shut and came back in. We sat on the couch, and he comforted me to the point where I fell asleep in his arms.

Over time we became closer, and I found myself depending on him for his steady comfort and strength, as I found myself emotionally weak during that stage in life. I'd been an independent woman for so many years until that point, but the presence of Lawrence made me lean on someone more than I ever imagined. I enjoyed it. We became lovers. I felt completely protected; having this lovely man in my house.

One day, unexpectedly, Lawrence knocked on my door and asked to come in. The worried look on his face reminded me of a schoolboy about to get in trouble. The trouble was soon to be mine, however, as he told me that he must break off our love affair because he met a younger woman. I was truly heartbroken.

As time passed, I thought more of the good times we had versus that awful news he told me while on my doorstep. He was a wonderful man with a good heart and cared for me during my most vulnerable and frightening moments. I wrote him to tell him that.

Oliver

Oliver was incredibly tender and kind. Tall and lanky, he was eight years my junior, and although I enjoyed the attention of a younger man, at moments I felt awkward and too old for him. When I met him, I had no interest in men and was still feeling the tender sting of the heartbreak inflected by Lawrence some years earlier.

I met Oliver while sitting at the bakery shop waiting for my order. This young man sat at my table and introduced himself as Oliver and asked if he could join me. I was very much caught off guard, you see, so I reluctantly agreed. Something was charming about his youthfulness that I couldn't resist, so I continued to talk with the man and agreed to meet him that Saturday evening for dinner at a restaurant of my choice.

We met for dinner and had a delightful time together. He spoke with such ease and sincerity. His blue eyes would twinkle every time he smiled. Oliver would make a point of doing something special for me a least once a week. Oh, I let it be known that I enjoyed fine things, but he always surprised me with a simple gesture: an evening out, flowers, or a simple lovely comment that warmed my heart. I have to say, I wasn't always the kindest to him. My body was changing, and when I felt insecure about how I looked, I lashed out at him as if he was going to reject me later. He would always reassure me of my beauty, and I will forever love the kindness he gave me.

We continued to see each other for several months, but by the third month, I came to realize that I was attracted to him as a person but pushed down the thought of being with him intimately as the desire never surfaced. I knew this would come up eventually. One afternoon, Oliver came to have dinner and afterward took my hand and asked if I desired him. I knew at that very moment that my answer was no, but for fear of crushing the young man, I said yes and escorted him upstairs.

Once in my room, Oliver asked if he could watch as I undressed. I bashfully agreed and did so until my last items of clothing; my brassier and underpants. I then took Oliver's hand, brought him to my bed, and asked him to lie beside me. I reached over and touched his face, told him how much I loved him, but I could not make love to him. He composedly collected his things and went on his way. I, of course, never heard from him again. Oliver was a lonely man when I met him, and I broke his heart that day.

I wrote Oliver to express how, after so many years, he had left an imprint on my soul. To have left such an impact, I truly believe, meant that he is a special man who has the incredible ability to warm a heart when it can be cold and lifeless. Oliver rejuvenated my faith in good men, and I will never forget the beautiful effect he had at that moment in my life.

Stephen

I was introduced to Stephen while at an anniversary party held by the mayor. Because I wrote articles for the local newspaper about the town's history, the mayor sent me an invitation to a gala event. The mayor and I were well acquainted, but he had an agenda that evening. Within moments of arriving, he introduced me to Stephen. He was a retired university professor and made quite the conversation! This man held my attention for the entire evening.

The retired professor had many friends and was known in many social circles in town and the big city. He invited me to many events; quite a few of them were out of town. I was certainly not accustomed to such a large number of social gatherings, as I lived a very private life up until that time. Having said that, I thoroughly enjoyed our evenings out because Stephen was such a good companion and gentleman.

Over the course of the six months, we were together, he introduced me to a countless number of people! I enjoyed how he was respected. I loved the way he made me feel special even when speaking with multiple people in one evening and never forgetting to introduce me. There were many evenings when Stephen had me laughing all evening long, and I vividly remember waking up the next morning with stomach pains from the laughter the night before. He was a brilliant, witty man who enjoyed entertaining. The six months we were together were a whirlwind of excitement.

Sadly, at some point by the end of our time together, I began to get tired of the evenings out, and Stephen continued to attend many social events on his own and eventually came home later and later and on several occasions, not at all. He expressed that he was hurt by what he felt was abandonment and began to drink and stay out more. I felt guilty for letting him down, as this wasn't my lifestyle. I was truly a small-town girl. We tried several times to have a nice evening out, but it was unnatural, and we soon drifted apart without even a formal goodbye.

I wrote Stephen to tell him that I have many fond memories of our time together and expressed how much of a wonderful companion and gentleman he was. I also reminded him of a saying he often told me which I repeated to myself in my later years, "Life is about making memories."

Mary never saw the letters but soon after being by Geraldine's side wrote a memoir of the woman's story.

One evening when Geraldine was getting worse, she called for Mary to come see her. She did as she was asked and sat beside her friend one last time. Geraldine told her to fetch the atlas that was in the reading room beside the globe. Although perplexed, Mary retrieved it and held it on her lap until the ailing woman opened her eyes again. Geraldine pointed to the atlas and told Mary to look inside the pages for a letter.

Mary flipped through the pages to find a single-page letter addressed to a Timothy. The ailing woman told Mary that there was another lover in her life whom she met when she was in her mid-fifties. She met Timothy two years after her relationship with Stephen ended. With Geraldine becoming increasingly tired, she asked Mary to send the letter to Timothy. She further explained that she wrote the letter to him but procrastinated over sending it.

Geraldine died a few days after the discovery of the letter but unfortunately never explained the reason why she was hesitant in sending it.

The reason why I know this story is because uncle Tom became friends with Mary after my uncle's wife passed away. Mary not only kept a memoir of

Geraldine's lovers, but she kept the letter to Timothy, as she could not find where this man lived or anything about him. The woman kept the story of Geraldine's three lovers and the letter secret for all of her life, but as she became older, she asked for uncle Tom's help in finding who this man might be, as this was Geraldine's last wish.

My uncle Tom did some research in the city's archives and death records, but he wasn't able to get very far, as no one ever knew Timothy's last name. Unfortunately, nothing ever came of Timothy or his whereabouts. Before Mary passed away, she gave her memoir and the letter to uncle Tom to keep.

The unshaven man paused and gulped down the remainder of his beer.

"What became of the letter?" I asked.

"Well," the old man said, as his eyes drilled into mine. "I have it now."

The man reached into his left pocket and took out a paper. He gently unfolded it and handed it to me.

"But..." He hesitated. "No one here can read it. Only you. You must read it so that I can hear what the letter said," he expressed, sneaking a glance at the two men at the bar.

I read it.

Dear Timothy,

I'm writing this letter after several earlier failed attempts. As the years pressed on, things for me became clearer, and as many say; time heals all wounds. It was difficult to accept that our time together had finished, and it saddens me even to this day that it ended so abruptly. I write you this letter for several reasons: to tell you how I feel as life's end for me is nearer, but I'm also writing this letter so that it may help console me while I reveal how you changed my life.

First of all, I want to tell you I've never regretted a moment with you as my world would certainly not have been the same if we had never met. I have never known anyone quite like you. You touched me in so many ways. I don't think this letter will ever give our love affair its proper justice. After all these years, I still miss you terribly. Some of the things I've experienced, I experienced only with you. I only knew passion with you.

It seemed however that, with that passion, came hurt. If I were to take away the pain, then I would have to give away that passion I experienced. That is why I have had difficulty keeping you in my thoughts for so many years. You see, I've had to push the memory of you far away, far down so that I wouldn't consciously think of you.

It worked. It worked until I would see a garden in the park or hear a song you first played for me, or I would mistakenly feel the touch of the inside of my arm that would remind me of you, even the smell of you. Once in a while, I would pass by a stranger who wore the same cologne. The moment of excitement would be quickly extinguished upon realizing it wasn't you.

I recall a time when we were at that small café in the middle of summer. You may not remember it the same as I did, but let me tell you how I recall it. We were seated at a small table on a bright sunny summer afternoon. You were staring out at the garden across from the café. I knew your mind was elsewhere and I felt distant from you. I called your name to get your attention, and you turned to me and smiled. You said: "Geraldine, there is a song that I will play for you when we get back home. I was thinking of it just now."

When you explained what you were thinking, you caressed my arm. You sat there, running your fingers up and down my arm from the crease of my elbow to my wrist. You studied it, and then you gazed into my eyes with your beautiful ones.

You were here with me. But then, I could see a sort of sadness as if you were drifting away again, even though the gentle touch of your fingertips melted away any hostility I had for you for not giving me your attention moments before.

Later that afternoon, you did play me that song. It was Debussy's "Arabesque No.1," something I can barely listen to now as it reminds me of you and makes me cry. It puts me in mind of that afternoon. I cannot recall feeling more alive than that day. I had no idea how I could feel as a woman until I met you. I may never have heard that beautiful music if I hadn't been introduced to it by you. These things all come to me.

You were a complicated man, and because I didn't understand you, there were many times I felt like I hated you for it. In fact, I did tell you I hated you. Yes. I'm sure you remember. I meant to hurt you when I said it.

It wasn't you I hated. I despised that I wasn't getting all of your attention when I wanted it. I resented the fact that I loved you more than you loved me, or so it seemed. It was my jealousy I couldn't stand. It tore me up and further distanced you from me.

As years passed on, I then felt guilty for telling you I hated you and that I wished I never met you. Nothing could be further from the truth. I just wanted you to say you loved me, but you never did. I wanted your attention always, but you didn't give it.

Other men before you did, and that's what made it difficult. Those other men weren't you, though, Timothy. There were times when you would walk through my front door, take me to the front room sofa and have your way with me without saying a word. You wanted me so badly; I soaked it in and felt as if I were in heaven. It made me feel desirable. Every woman would want that. I can still feel your touch and its sensations to this day. Oh, how I enjoyed you!

I've come to understand that my hostility towards you was actually against me and my impatience. You were never mean or distrustful towards me. It was your distant nature that frustrated me. I'm sorry for saying those horrible things.

I've come to accept that you were a lost soul. Your admiration for life shifted moment by moment and within a moment; I felt like I lost you. A new sensation would take you off into a different world and to me, you were miles away. I can see that you struggled with being grounded. I've accepted that now. One day you will no longer be lost. It will come to you when you are ready. Thank you, Timothy, for being in my life. Being with you was a very special time for me. Thank you for making memories.

Geraldine

At that point, I folded the letter and handed it back to the unshaven man.

"Thank you!" he said with gratitude.

"Thank you for the whiskey." I grabbed my beer and returned to the bar.

The man with the glasses was still keeping his eyes on me. He didn't appear to be judging but just wondering why I was there.

"One more for the road!" the bartender said as he slapped down another shot of whiskey.

"Am I going somewhere?"

The bartender didn't answer right away but seemed as if he wanted to say something.

"Why is it you can read these letters with those glasses?" he asked.

"I don't know."

"Well . . . It's time to hand them over." He spoke with an authoritative tone. "Before you do, take that shot of whiskey. It's on the house. You did well, my friend."

I sat there for a moment and wondered what I did "well." I felt a little sad thinking I arrived there, had one beer and three shots of whiskey, and accomplished nothing to help out my lost friend . . . Or did I?

I downed the shot and closed my eyes as I took the glasses off and placed them on the bar. I kept them closed as the burning of the whiskey made its way down to my stomach.

I felt the air around me change and a breeze pick up; my lungs filled with the fresh air. It was cool but refreshing. I felt this strange heat around my feet, so I open my eyes to witness the Golden Retriever sitting at them, panting and looking up at me.

"Hello, boy. You came back!" I leaned over to pet him.

I was no longer in the stale air of that dark dank pub. I was on the bench looking out at the trees!

"Come on, boy!" I called as I stood.

The dog jumped up and headed back down the path toward where we came from.

The path twisted and turned much like it did on the way in until we reached John St. where the streetlight lit it up. Beside the rock was the red balloon hovering in mid-air as it did previously. Dangling from it was a note bundled up as it was before. I sat on the rock, but before I opened the package, I called the dog over because he was standing in the middle of the road.

"Here, boy!" I called again, but he didn't come. He kept looking back down the street as if to indicate that was where he was going. He turned and headed towards the north side. The clicking of his nails dissipated as he galloped down the street until I couldn't see or hear him anymore.

I unraveled the note. As soon as I let go of the string, the red balloon lifted high up in the air, up over the trees of the ravine until it was out of sight. I opened the letter and it simply said:

```
Thank you!
```

Part 3

The Typewriter

Friday, July 20, 1984, 3:04 a.m.

Click, click, click, clack, click, click, click, click clack . . . I heard as I slowly opened my eyes to the darkness in my room. *I hear it! I hear it way off in the distance.* I took my clock and placed it under my pillow. Yes, I heard it clearly, that click, click, click, clack sound. I got out of bed and opened the drapes to see John St. lit up by the streetlight. *It sounds like a typewriter. Who would be writing at this time of night?* I went back to my bed, took the clock from underneath my pillow, placed it on the night table, and closed my eyes.

Tick, tick, tick, tick, ...click, click, click, clack, click, click, click, click, clack . . . tick, tick, tick, tick . . . click, click, click, clack, click, clack . . . click, click, click, clack, click tick, tick, tick, tick, . . . click, click, click, clack . . . .

All right. Enough of this! Off I went with my shoes in hand.

As I made my way down the hill, to the rock, I cocked my head to one side so that I could take in where the noise was coming from. The sound echoed, but after I did another 360, I determined it was coming from the ravine.

I crossed the street towards the dense bush of the ravine in the direction of this typewriter sound. Once at the bushes, I closed my eyes, covered them with my hands, and pushed my way through. The dense bush scratched my forearms as I pushed through, which stung a little. I finally made my way through to the clearing where I could see the stream. *I have seen the stream many times before, but I've never seen that bridge.* As I approach the old stone bridge over the stream, I could hear it again . . . click, click, click, clack, click, click, click, click clack. It was a little louder. As I passed over the rocky surface, I thought I heard a voice coming from underneath. At that moment, the clickety-clack of the typewriter stopped. *I must have been hearing things. I'm sure I heard a voice!* By the time I reached the other side, the click, clack of the typewriter started again.

The path over the bridge narrowed onto a dirt pathway into the forest, tightening into a denser area of poplar and pine trees. Along the dirt pathway through the tall pines, I enjoyed the crisp smell. The typewriter became increasingly louder as I headed deeper into the wilderness that blocked out any light from the night sky, but I wanted to see where this noise was coming from. It didn't make sense why someone would be typing in the middle of the night in the dark woods.

A faint glow broke out from the tallest trees. I picked up my pace, encouraged by the small light coming from a cottage in the middle of the clearing. I made my way around the cottage, which had unusually large windows, to spy a bald middle-aged man hunched over his desk typewriter. He wore dark sunglasses. A lit cigarette sat in his ashtray, its stream of smoke lifting into the air.

As I neared the side window, I could see him typing and typing, but there was no paper in his typewriter! He reached for his cigarette. Seeing his face still straight ahead, I realized that the man was blind. He took a drag and then exhaled. Lifting his chin as he did. He put the cigarette down and smiled to himself as if a thought just came to mind and began typing again. Click, click, click, clack. The noise was rather loud and irritating.

It didn't make sense why this man would be toiling without any paper. I wanted to walk up to his front door and ask him if he was aware that he was just working on the roller versus paper, but I'm sure he knew what he was doing. In any case, I didn't want to disturb him, and it certainly wasn't any of my business. I'm not sure what the purpose of all this was, and I certainly didn't have the heart to tell him to stop making so much noise with his dammed typewriter in the middle of the night. *Why am I the only one this is bothering? I'm sure light sleepers on my street could hear this. Maybe it's just me.*

I paced the cottage a few times thinking of ways how I could let this man know that he was making noise and not accomplishing anything but decided to leave him alone and made my way back along the path.

The click, clack of the typewriter weakened as I casually strolled through the forest. I stopped for a moment, turned back to study the cottage and the faint light in the window. I felt sad for the man because whatever it was that he was smiling about, whatever it was that he was typing, was disappearing with every stroke of the key. I resumed my journey. The click, clack wasn't as disturbing as when I stood outside the cottage. It was almost like the sound of a woodpecker far off in the distance.

As I approached the bridge, the click, clack faded, and I could hear a man's voice from beneath the bridge. I stopped for a moment and turned around to see if the man's voice was coming from the cottage, but it wasn't. I made my way down the embankment to see who was down there. I could hear it. It said --

". . . a very quiet man he was. He had a slender build and a sunken face with high cheekbones. He had dark hair combed to one side and . . ."

I made my way farther down the embankment and then underneath to the hollow, expecting to see a man sitting in it beside the stream, but there was no man. It was an echo of a voice from somewhere else that became louder and clearer the closer I was to the stone arch.

"He wore a brown suit that was far too big for his slender frame. He was clean-shaven and had this odor of freshly sprinkled cheap aftershave."

I turned to climb back up the hill to see where the man's voice came from, but the clarity and volume diminished slightly farther up to the top of the bridge. Towards the cottage, the voice was completely gone, but the click, clack was clear. I paced back and forth between the bridge and the cottage.

It's the typewriter talking! The man in the cottage is talking through his typewriter.

"This poor man. This is the story of the forgotten man."

I took a few steps down the embankment, closer to the hollow, and sat to listen to this man's story as he typed.

The man in a brown suit had come in to see Mr. Flanagan. He approached the front desk where Mrs. Wilson was stationed.

"Hello." He smiled. "I'm here to see Mr. Flanagan. I was given his name by his friend, Paul Bannister."

"I'll let him know you are here Mr. . . .?" Mrs. Wilson asked. "Henry. Thomas Henry," the man responded.

"Is he expecting you?"

"I believe so."

"Please take a seat?"

The man sat on a wooden bench beside the entrance as Mrs. Wilson walked behind her desk to the back offices and finally returned.

"Mr. Henry. Mr. Flanagan wasn't expecting you, but he will give you fifteen minutes. He is just in a meeting at the moment," she said as she took her seat

"Thank you!"

Thomas Henry waited patiently for an hour, rather still the entire time perusing the wall in front of him. Mrs. Wilson went to the back offices again and then returned, followed by a tall man in a black suit.

"Mister . . ." he asked while stretching out his hand.

"Henry."

"Mr. Henry." He paused with a puzzled look on his face. "My apologies, but I don't recall anyone telling me you were coming. Who was it that asked you to come see me?"

"Mr. Paul Bannister."

"Paul Bannister. Yes, I know him quite well. He's an old friend of mine." He paused again. "But I'm sorry . . ." he said, placing his right forefinger and thumb on his forehead while shaking it. "I don't recall Paul mentioning you coming to see me." He then brought his hand down to his chin. "I tell you what. Give me a little more time, as I have a call to make, and I'll have Mrs.

Wilson bring you in shortly after," he said, now smiling.

"That's fine," Thomas replied and proceeded to sit.

"Mr. Flanagan?" Mrs. Wilson asked as he walked by. "Just a reminder. I have to take my mother to the doctor's this afternoon and won't be back until tomorrow morning."

"Yes, Dorothy. Don't worry. I didn't forget!" he said as he walked back to his office.

Mrs. Wilson meticulously packed her purse and made quick steps out the door.

All along, the man on the wooden bench waited patiently for Mr. Flanagan to come to the front of the office. He waited until the sun went down. There were moments when he considered entering the back office but didn't want to disturb anyone, as he knew how busy and important Mr. Flanagan was.

Thomas removed his jacket, hung it up on the coat hanger on the other side of the office, and proceeded to sit patiently on the wooden bench.

The man continued sitting in his dull blue dress shirt but eventually grew tired, so he leaned his left arm on the armrest of the wooden bench and placed his head on his hand, closed his eyes, and fell asleep.

As the sun rose, the man woke and realized he'd spent the entire night in the office, so he rushed to the men's room to wash his face and comb his hair. He returned to the bench, opened a stick of gum, and chewed it to freshen his breath.

Moments later, Mrs. Wilson arrived.

"Good morning! You're back."

Feeling embarrassed to admit that he had waited the entire night, Thomas replied: "Good morning!"

Moments later, Mr. Flanagan appeared from the back office, and, once seeing the man, stopped in surprise.

"Oh?"

"Ummm. Yes, sir." Mr. Henry replied. "I thought I'd better come back today as you seemed occupied yesterday."

"I see," Rather puzzled.

"Mr. Flanagan," Mrs. Wilson said, to get his attention.

"Yes, Dorothy," he replied softly while pointing his left ear toward her.

"The front door was left unlocked last night. . ." she whispered under her breath "and this man was there when I arrived."

The two continued to his office.

A few minutes later, Mrs. Wilson returned. "Mr. Flanagan will be with you in a few minutes," she said with a forced smile.

Thomas Henry waited once more, this time for forty-five minutes.

Two police officers entered the office. One of them stood at the front desk, observing the man on the bench while the other one inquired about Mr. Flanagan. Moments later, he was led to the back office. The man on the bench sat still keeping to himself, thinking that this Mr. Flanagan must be quite the busy man now that he has to deal with the police.

The second man in uniform leaned against Mrs. Wilson's desk, observing Thomas Henry.

Fifteen minutes passed, and out came the second man in uniform with Mr. Flanagan. The man in uniform approached Mr. Henry.

"May I ask your name, sir?"

"It's Thomas Henry. Is there a problem, sir?" the man inquired.

"Yes. There appears to be. Please come with us to the police station for some questions."

"Of course. I can't imagine what the problem would be. May I collect my jacket?"

Once at the police station, the man explained the scenario as to what happened the day before and that he had fallen asleep waiting. The police officers took down their notes and asked the man to wait outside on the wooden bench until they contacted Mr. Flanagan and would call upon him once they had more questions. It was about noon and the man on the bench was feeling weak as he had nothing to eat since the morning before, but he didn't say anything, as he felt he had already caused enough commotion for one day.

The man on the bench sat in the police station and looked out at the street witnessing pedestrians rush by as the afternoon sun pierced through the window. One of the two officers left the office and eventually returned with lunch for several others.

Two hours had passed by, and the man on the bench observed both men in uniform bustle to and from their offices. Once in a while, Thomas would hear laughter come from one of the police officers.

Thomas Henry waited and waited until late in the afternoon when one of the men in uniform passed by and stopped suddenly.

"Oh. Yes . . . Mr. . . .?"

"Henry," the man answered for him.

"Yes, well . . . uh. You are clear to go now."

The man on the bench took his jacket that was folded neatly on his lap and stood. He intended to head directly to a restaurant but suddenly became weak. He fell to his knees, then to his chest, and finally banging his head. Three men from the station rushed towards him.

"Sir. Are you all right?" one of the men asked as they picked him up.

"What happened?" the man asked as he came to.

"You fell and banged your head. You must have passed out." The man in uniform then turned his head towards the front desk and yelled: "Can we get him an icepack please?"

The men took him back to the wooden bench to set him down. An administrator brought ice wrapped in a towel to place on his head.

After a few minutes, two of these men encouraged the man to stand and wrap his arms around their shoulders as they walked him to a nearby police car. They gingerly placed him in the back of it and drove him to a hospital where they stopped at Emergency, collected a wheelchair, and pushed him into the waiting area. One man stayed with Thomas, while the other spoke with the hospital administrator.

"What happened to me?" the man in the wheelchair asked.

"You fell and banged your head, sir."

"Yes, but . . ." he paused. "But, why was I in the police station?"

"You don't remember? Mr. Flanagan thought you broke into his office last night. We brought you in for questioning."

"Oh." Thomas held the ice pack on his head. "Why would I do a thing like that?"

"Well, we came to the conclusion that you were being honest when you said you must have slept through the night while waiting for Mr. Flanagan. We rang him, and he confirm he forgot about you yesterday and agreed to drop the whole thing," the man in uniform said, in a kindly tone.

"Oh, yes. Mr. Flanagan," The man in the wheelchair said with a slight grin. "I had a very good business proposition for him. Paul Bannister suggested that I pass it along to his old friend." He grinned to himself. "Mr. Randal Flanagan," continued the man. "He won't be getting my lead. No, I've got a better idea," he said, keeping his cheery expression intact.

Once the other man in uniform was finished with the administrator, he approached the man in the wheelchair.

"They'll be with you shortly, sir. Just relax and leave that icepack on your forehead," he said sweetly and carried on to the police car with the other man in uniform. The officers took off in their car.

The man in the wheelchair looked around while patients came in and out of the hospital. As he continued to wait, he became very hungry and just wanted a bowl of soup and a cup of coffee.

After an hour passed, a nurse approached. "Hello, sir," the woman said, bending down to make eye contact.

"Yes," he said, his face angled up at her enticingly, hoping he may finally get that bowl of soup.

"We need that wheelchair. Would you mind sitting on the bench, please?"

"Ahh. Ok. Yes." He glanced around as he got off the chair and sat on the bench. The ice pack was completely melted, and he was just holding a cold wet towel.

The nurse took the chair and rolled it down the hallway.

As the man on the bench sat, he witnessed patient after patient come and go into the observation room. A doctor would enter one room and then leave to go to another and eventually arrive back at the original room.

Thomas Henry had enough. He stood, exited the hospital, and sauntered down the street to a café to get that bowl of soup and cup of coffee that he had been wanting.

The voice stopped. I waited for a moment but didn't hear anything. I got to my feet and started towards

the small cottage to see if I could hear the clickety-clack of the typewriter: but nothing.

I was feeling tired, so I made my way across the bridge, through the dense bushes, across the street, and back home to bed.

Monday, July 23, 1984, 3:11 am

Click, click, click, clack, click . . . I heard as my eyes opened. I hear it. I heard that sound again. *The man and the typewriter are at it again. He has another story for me.*

Down I went towards John St. I brought a jacket to avoid the scratches from the bushes. It had been a couple of days since I was awakened by that sound. I either slept through it or that man in the cottage hadn't been composing.

I made my way through the bushes, holding my arms up, and my jacket stopped the scratching of my forearms as it did a few nights ago. Click, click, click I heard through the woodlands towards the little house. The sound became louder as I made my way toward the bridge.

I could hear it. The voice, under the bridge.

". . . that's when I first felt it. It was there, although it was in the distance. I felt it."

I hiked down the embankment and sat as I had the other night.

"At first, I only felt it once or twice a year. I was in my early twenties. One evening, I was lying in bed, tired, but my mind was occupied. Just as I was about to fall asleep, I felt it: the presence of something off in the distance. It didn't frighten me. Not an excited feeling, it was like something patiently waiting for me, but, as I said, while I was in my twenties, it was far away. That's the best I could explain it.

One day when I was in my mid-thirties, happily married, with young children running around the house, I escaped upstairs to take a nap, as I was exhausted, and my wife was reading a story for the kids. It was peaceful.

I closed my eyes, and just as I was about to drift off, there it was again -- that feeling, the feeling of it, but this time it was a little closer. I can't tell you how I knew it was nearer, but it was. I felt that whatever it was -- was still patient. This time, I could almost see it. But then again; I couldn't describe it.

Life kept going on for me. The children became older, and my wife and I did the best we could to raise them. While in my mid-forties, life became tough, and I wasn't making very much money. We were in the middle of an economic downturn. I worked for an engineering firm that had hired me five years earlier with very little experience, but they were very good to me when I was first hired. During the recession, the owner of the company decided to cut everyone's pay by 20% rather than lay off any employees. This made life tough for many of us, but I stuck it out.

One day, while I was enjoying a pint of beer after work, a gentleman introduced himself as a representative from another engineering firm from the other side of the city. We talked for a bit, and I was hopeful that he may offer me a job with a higher salary. This man didn't offer me a salary increase. However, he made me an offer that was very good financially. Still . . . there were strings attached.

The offer was that he would honor the same salary but would give me $7,000 in cash if I found a way to bring, from my current employer, specific drawings that would benefit his company. Well, I couldn't give him an answer at that very moment, and he told me to think on it for a few days. $7,000 was a lot of money at that time. I decided not to tell my wife of the offer as I felt a little ashamed at the thought of entertaining it, but I didn't tell the gentleman "no" either.

I didn't sleep that night and woke up angry that, of all the opportunities I had hoped would come my way, this is the only one that presented itself that would directly benefit me. But the offer definitely would have caused problems for the owner of my current company. I didn't wait long, so, early the next morning, I rang up the man whom I met at the bar and told him, "No thank you."

I carried on with work and never told my wife of the proposition. I had many discouraging days as money was tight, and I kept the man's number. I even picked up the phone to call him, but I quickly changed my mind and hung up. I couldn't do it. It wasn't right, no matter how desperate things seemed to be.

My wife and I made it through those tough financial times, and I never looked back at that offer.

Life went on and I began to get older and my children became adults and eventually moved out of the house one by one. I was then in my late fifties and I was beginning to understand what life was like living in a house with one person. We had our challenges as a couple, and I've found the patience in my midlife that I didn't have when I was in my twenties and thirties.

It was early in the morning while my wife was still sleeping, and the sun was just peeking through the sky. I felt its warmth. I still couldn't see it sharply, but it was a light glow hovering in the distance. I remember that when I closed my eyes, I could see it clearly but not when they were open.

Ten years passed. Shortly after I retired from the engineering firm, my wife became ill and passed away seven months later. I was then sixty-eight and faced with living the rest of my life alone. I struggled with this incredible loss. I had never known my father, and I was never close to my mother; therefore, this was the greatest loss I had ever experienced. I began to doubt life and its meaning and pondered why I was even placed on this earth. It was a lonely pain, and I was guilty about not appreciating the time with my wife while she was alive and well. I guess I never "counted my blessings," as the saying goes.

Very early one morning, I was suddenly awakened. It was too early to get up and too late to expect a full night's sleep. I closed my eyes and there it was again: the glow. Seeing it made me smile. It was there as it always had been, but clearer.

When I opened my eyes, I felt it without seeing it. This strange feeling provided a sort of comfort and gave me reason to continue on with life even though at times I questioned why I needed to. After that occurrence, I saw things differently. I saw enjoyment in life and in others, which strengthened my desire to keep going.

I often reflected on my experiences. I remembered the wonderful moments I had from my youth on to adulthood and on to my later years. I ruminated on the mistakes, and although I regretted them, I realized I needed to forgive myself and move on, making every effort not to repeat them. I found that reality has funny ways of throwing curveballs to test you. I also pondered the tough decisions that came my way and how grateful I was for the strength I had to make the right ones.

Early one evening after spending the afternoon clearing out my garden for the year, I was fatigued from the ordeal, so I sat on my usual chair, closed my eyes, and there it was again. It was right there. I was in its presence. I felt it. I could see it. It was like seeing a familiar face, but it had none. It was so comforting; it gave me the same warmth I would feel from returning home from a long trip or the feeling of slipping into a warm bed after spending hours out in the cold evening. While I embraced this new journey, I took in the beautiful scenery. The air was pleasant and odorless. There was a sweet sound of something, but it wasn't music. My body felt weightless. I knew I was far away from where I was, but I wasn't frightened or lonely.

The voice stopped. I didn't hear anything more. After lifting my head, I turned left and right to make sure my ears were tuned in properly. I stood and climbed the hill. I proceeded towards the small cottage, but I didn't hear anything from the typewriter. I hesitated, almost turning back towards home, but kept going.

I made my way through the pines and poplar trees. I could see the small light from the tiny cottage. I neared it, and still no clickity-clack from the typewriter. I walked around to the side window and could see the middle-aged man sitting back in his chair, taking long drags from his cigarette with his head back while thinking. He seemed content and relaxed. He poured what looked like a glass of whiskey and downed it quickly. I walked back home that night, thinking of what may be going through the mind of that man on the typewriter.

Tuesday, July 24, 1984, 3:09 am

Tick, tick, tick, tick . . . that's what I heard when I opened my eyes. . . The tick, tick of my clock. It was almost ten after three in the morning, and I didn't hear the clickety-clack of the typewriter. This was fine with me as I'd rather fall back asleep, so I closed my eyes and thought of pleasant things to calm my mind and drift back to sleep, but it didn't work. I was too preoccupied with the man and his typewriter. *What could be wrong? I hope he is OK. Maybe he drank too much. Why don't I hear anything?*

I took my shoes, and out I went, down the hill, across the street, through the bushes, and across the bridge. Still no clickety-clack of the typewriter. When I made it to the cottage, I was afraid of what I might see, but I did peek through the window to spy the middle-aged man sitting in front of his typewriter. His hands were under his black glasses and over his eyes while the stream of cigarette smoke twirled in the air. The thought of going up and knocking on the door crossed my mind, but I just couldn't. I could tell the man was in a deep-thinking mode.

I'm not sure why, but I felt sorry for him. Maybe he was suffering from writer's block. Just as I was about to move, he dropped his hands and glanced out at the window toward me.

I froze!

I stood there like a fool not knowing what to do. He picked up his cigarette, took a long drag, let it out, turned to his typewriter, and began typing. I headed toward the bridge. The click, click, click clack of the typewriter made my heart race in anticipation of his next story. I quickened my pace to not miss anything. I made it to the bridge and could hear the click, click, click, clack transpose to . . .

. . . The night air was clear, and I could hear the trickle of the water splashing as it passed the rocks. The water level rose inch by inch as I watched the stream from the embankment. The stream eventually rose about a foot, and from behind me, I could hear a voice: a man calling out from up the stream. Suddenly from underneath the bridge appeared this man on a small boat with a lantern . . .

There he was! The man in a small boat with an oil lantern appeared from underneath the bridge, just as the man on the typewriter's story said. *I* was in the story!

"Hello, young fella," the man in the boat said as he pushed his oar against the bank of the stream to stop the boat.

I paused for a moment.

"Sir?" I replied with a puzzled tone.

"Here is your boat . . . and your lantern," he continued as he got out of it and held it by the rope.

"I didn't hire a boat, sir. You must be mistaken."

"There's no mistake. It was ordered for you."

"It was?" I was still stunned by what was happening.

I contemplated the boat and the man holding the rope in one hand and the lantern in the other. He was elderly with white stubble on his face and hair scattered around the sides of his head. His expression was pleasant. His eyes had an unusual twinkle in them. They looked familiar, somehow. The boat banged against the rocks.

"Come on, lad. The water is getting impatient. You have quite a journey ahead of you," he said jauntily.

As I passed the man to regard the boat, I could smell stale whiskey and cigarettes on his breath.

"In you go!"

I brought one foot over the gunwale and the other and finally sat on the bench.

"Your oars are right there if you need them." He pointed. "You'll need one to guide you once in a while. Here's your lantern." He handed it to me. "Good luck." The man graciously placed the rope just inside the bow and gave the rowboat a push with his foot.

The old man waved as it drifted at a slow pace down the stream that widened, carrying it through the waterway. The stream became a slow-moving river. I studied the treed shoreline which eventually disappeared and the river opened into a large body of water. The water became very still, and the boat just sat motionless. The light from the lantern cast a reflection onto the water, but not far enough to see beyond a hundred feet or so. I studied the flame as it flickered inside the lantern.

I lifted it but still couldn't see anything. I remained for some time and considered taking the oars out to get moving when I noticed a slight ripple. A breeze picked up and the ripples became greater. The boat began to move. I placed the lantern closer to me to make sure it didn't tip.

The wind took the boat farther and farther away — from where, I wasn't sure, as I'd lost the sense of what direction I came from. The boat rocked back and forth, so I held the lantern tightly. The warm wind picked up, and I could tell by the tiny bit of light reflecting that the boat was moving faster. This continued until I felt a thud. The boat suddenly stopped.

I lifted the lantern to gain a full perspective of a sandy beach. I swung my arm back and forth to get a better view of where I was.

I stepped out of the boat and pulled it up onto the sand. I started towards a boardwalk, which was surrounded by lush green grass. It creaked and snapped. It eventually ended at a set of wooden stairs that led up to what looked like a small tavern. I could see a faint orange light shine through the window from inside.

I ascended the stairs and took in the fresh air along the squeaky oak steps. The breeze was quite nice as it blew my hair from side to side

When I arrived at the tavern, I poked my head in front of one of the windows to spy an interesting-looking man working behind the bar; the entire top was scattered with burning candles. I opened the door and entered, seeing another man at the bar holding a piece of paper in hand.

The bartender had very short hair and a large mustache that almost covered his mouth.

The man sitting at the bar had dark brown hair and was scanning the piece of paper until I walked in. He lifted his head. At first, he had a very serious expression, and then his demeanor lit up as he realized, just as I did, that we looked identical. I was astonished! This man looked exactly like me! He placed the paper on the bar, stood, and stretched out his hand.

"I knew I had a twin," he said with a big smile. "Wow! Finally. I meet you!" He gave me a firm handshake. "Come." He gestured to the chair beside him. "Have a seat." He turned to the man with the large mustache. "Fred, give the man a drink, please. Put it on my tab."

The bartender peered at me with a plain face as he waited for my answer.

"A beer, please."

"You can put your lantern on the bar," he said pleasantly.

I did.

The man turned to look at me, then at my twin, and then back.

"Beer huh?" my twin commented. "I prefer wine myself. Pour me a little more please, Fred."

The man behind the bar nodded and prepared our drinks. My twin turned to me.

"Cheers!"

"Cheers!"

I took advantage of the moment to study his face. He was identical. It was eerie. He finished his sip and picked up the piece of paper he was holding earlier.

"You are probably wondering what this is." He gestured to the paper.

"A little. What is it if I may ask?"

"Come closer and I'll tell you," he whispered as I leaned in. "' see that lady over there?" he asked, tilting his head towards a woman sitting in the back corner near an unlit fireplace. "The letter I'm writing is for her."

"I don't understand" I stated. I leaned back.

"Let me tell you how it all started. A few months ago, I began to see that woman enter this tavern. She didn't come in regularly, but once in a while, she'd come in to read her book and enjoy her wine and cigarette. I was immediately attracted to her. One day I finally had the courage to say hello and asked her out on a date. To make a long story short, we dated for a few months, but it was rocky. We stopped seeing each other as both of our feelings were being hurt by the other's misunderstandings. The thing is, she will be going back home tomorrow. There is so much I want to say, but I can't say it face to face. I didn't expect her to be here tonight, so I am quite anxious, to say the least. I'm afraid of her leaving without having the chance to let her know how I really feel, so I decided to handwrite a letter on this paper that this fine gentleman at the bar gave me. This is my last chance."

"I see."

I peered behind the shoulders of my twin to spy the woman near the fireplace. She was smoking a very thin cigarette and reading a book she held open with her left hand; in her right, she held the cigarette with her elbow situated on the table. A glass of red wine was positioned in front. I could only see her side profile. Her straight brown hair was shoulder-length. The little bit of light from the candle exposed her lovely complexion.

She turned towards me briefly, and my heart began to race as her brown almond eyes aimed directly at mine for a brief moment and then turned back to her book. Feeling foolish, I cast my eyes away from hers and my face flushed, so I took a sip of my beer.

"How far did you get?" I asked with a slight tremble in my voice.

I became very distracted by the presence of this woman and had a difficult time focusing on my twin.

"I didn't start. I have an idea in my head, but it's silly and it doesn't come out right when I'm about to jot it down."

"Well . . ." I said with a slight hesitation, "why don't you tell me about your time together."

"Hmmm." His eyes shifted back and forth as he pondered the question. "She was a woman who inspired me. Our conversations were sometimes deep and thought-provoking She made me think of what else was outside of my little box of a world that I lived in. At the same time, I felt like she was able to feed off of what I had experienced in life, which I appreciated. We had great compatibility that way. Once in a while though . . ." He paused, and his face changed slightly as he spoke. "Something would come up and we couldn't talk it through and it hung in the room like stale air. This didn't happen all the time, but it had its way of coming up every once in a while. When we weren't together, I would reflect on those moments and I became even more distant and hurt, but at the same time, couldn't wait to see her. When I did, there was a magnetic pull as soon as we laid eyes on each other. The attraction was quite something."

He rubbed his forehead with his right hand. "It perplexed me because I believed . . . deep down inside, I loved her," he said as his hazel eyes fixated on mine. He let up and sat silent for a moment and eventually returned his attention to me. "Do you ever fight with your own emotions?"

"How so?" I asked.

As I listened, I took in this strange but sweet aroma of a distant perfume.

"I feel that I've made the mistake of not telling her that I think of her every day and sometimes every hour of every day, but there were times when I felt hurt and became defensive. Was it me? Or was it us?" He ran his hand along his forehead again. He struggled with whatever decision he had made. While he contemplated his thoughts, I looked over his shoulder again to see that the woman had gone; her lit cigarette still burning in the ashtray and her wine glass empty. It appeared that she had left while we were talking, but I didn't have the heart to tell him, as I could feel his pain already.

"Tell me some of the special things you had together," I asked, trying to take him out of his sad state.

"Hmmm." My twin thought for a moment with his hand pulling on his chin as if he had a goatee. "I can't tell you a specific event . . . or occasion. We had those, but it wasn't like that. It was her presence, her smile, the smell of her hair."

"Go on," I encouraged.

"When she smiled, her eyes lit up."

"And?"

"Her kisses were beautiful. Our deep kisses were incredibly sensual," he expressed as his eye contact broke from mine. "I enjoyed caressing her naked tummy, navel, hips, and thighs. When she was completely relaxed, she let me caress and kiss her neck while I pushed her brown hair away from it. Sometimes I enjoyed talking with her just to hear her accent and not take in anything she was saying. It was all of this, my twin. It was all of this. So, I sit here, trying to decide what to tell her, but all I do is stare at this blank piece of paper, torturing myself."

I sympathized with my twin, as I could feel his pain.

"Do you think . . ." I began to ask as my voice broke. "Excuse me." I cleared my throat. "Do you think that perhaps what you had is . . . what it is?" I said.

My twin appeared puzzled. "I don't know what you mean."

Worried that my questions may upset him I dismissed it. "Never mind. It was just a silly question."

"No. Repeat it. I have to face what it is that I'm struggling with."

"Perhaps it was meant to be what it is; a fiery, sensual relationship that may be as real and beautiful as it could be, but not necessarily a long one." I paused to think a moment. "Perhaps, the lifespan of your love affair was best to be short-lived. That doesn't mean it wasn't a strong one."

"I'm not so sure. As of right now, the pain is still there." He hesitated a moment, and a worried look came over his face. "She passed by us and left, didn't she?" He turned his head to see an empty table; the cigarette still burning.

"I . . . I didn't notice when she left."

My twin stood and strode to the table, grabbed the cigarette, and sat in front of me. He held the cigarette between his right thumb and forefinger and let the smoke swirl around my face. He held it in front of me. "Take a drag."

"Why?" I asked rather puzzled.

"Just try it," he said with persuasion

I took the thin cigarette, brought it to my mouth, inhaled it and when I exhaled, I stretched my neck out towards the ceiling. When I let my neck relax, the woman with the brown hair was seated in front of me where my twin was.

"See. It's smooth isn't it," she said with her accent. She looked pleased, reaching for it.

"Hello," I answered with a strange calmness.

Her almond eyes crinkled around the edges. I stared at her for a moment, even though I naturally wouldn't have. I studied her brown hair as it lightly touched her neck. I traced her lips with my eyes from end to end. I wanted to lean closer for a kiss, but I knew that couldn't happen. I became warm and anxious as I sat close to her. My heart raced again.

"Your twin can't make up his mind, can he?" she asked, taking a puff from her cigarette, then exhaling it from the side of her mouth. "You're not offering much help, either." She paused for a moment. "It's OK. You've made your choice." She passed the cigarette back.

I took it.

"He will miss you."

I took a drag from the cigarette and let it out into the air high into the ceiling as if to release the pain my twin was feeling. When I brought my head back, the woman with the brown hair was gone, the seat in front of me empty, and the cigarette crushed into the ashtray.

I sat for a moment, empty inside. The bartender had disappeared as well, so I took the lantern, left the tavern and carefully paced down the wooden steps, meandered along the boardwalk to the beach to find my boat. It was still dark, and the only light came from the lantern as it swung in my hand.

As I approached the boat, I noticed from the indentation in the sand that it had been moved closer to the water. I held the lantern up high to get a better view and spied my twin sitting in it with the oars out into the water.

"Hello again, my twin," the voice said from the boat. "I'm ready to take you home. Give us a push, will you!"

I placed the lantern on the seat and thrust the boat out into the water and stepped in. Once I sat, he pushed the oars forward, then pulled back to get us away from the beach. He didn't speak much as we made our way farther from where we were. The earlier breeze I experienced had since died.

"I have a question for you," he asked as he rowed.

"Yes."

"Are you having trouble sleeping, too?"

"Yes, as a matter of fact, I am."

He was silent after I answered as if he expected me to continue. I watched the oars lift out and dip back into the still water. The oars creaked as they swiveled. The pause was awkward.

"What is it that you think is keeping you up at night?" I asked to break the silence.

"Hmmm . . . I think that . . ." He paused for a moment. "I think that I think too much during the day."

"What is it you ponder?" I asked as I listened to the splashing.

"I believe that there's more to life than the day-to-day grind, therefore I daydream a lot. When I wake in the middle of the night, I feel more alive," he said as I watched the light shining on my twin's face as he pushed and pulled.

"Then . . ." He grunted a little as he pulled ". . . I think about the decisions I've made. Were they the right ones? Wrong ones? In fact." He grunted again as he pulled. "I have my regrets and I struggle with them too. The nighttime allows me to explore why." Then he chuckled to himself. "Sometimes . . . Sometimes I take a journey. I meet lots of people I would normally not have met during the day."

"Shall I take over?" I asked.

"No, no. I'm fine. We're almost there."

I raised the lantern high above my head, but I didn't see any land, so I placed it back.

I continued watching my twin row. He would let out the odd grunt, but still maintained a steady pace and didn't seem to lose energy. My eyes began to feel dry, so I gave them a rub to relieve them.

"You're getting tired, aren't you?" he asked.

"A little." I lied. I was feeling very tired.

"Have a look behind you."

I picked up the lantern, turned, and saw the opening of the stream. My twin pushed and pulled and adjusted his oars to navigate through the stream as it got narrower until the boat stopped, jolting my body back.

"Here you are."

Behind me, I saw the bridge and embankment where I sat the night before.

"Go to sleep. Get some rest before you get too weak. But leave the lantern. I'll need that to see where I'm going next."

I got out of the boat. It felt good to stretch my legs.

"Until we meet again," he said with a wave and then made his way under the bridge and up the stream.

I waved and ascended the embankment to the road. I stopped to listen, but I did not hear the click, click clack of the typewriter. I considered making the journey towards the tiny cottage to see if the man was OK, but my body was telling me to go to bed, which is exactly what I did.

Part 4

The Whispering Room

Friday, Nov. 2, 1984, 3:13 a.m.

I woke while lying on my back. I lay in bed very still, and as my eyes opened, I saw a bright red light shining through the window onto the ceiling of my room. I sat up, swung my legs from underneath my blankets, and darted to the window. I opened the drapes to view a hotel across the street where the ravine used to be.

The red neon light from the hotel sign was almost directly across from my window, which caused me to squint as I tried to make out the details of the hotel. As my eyes adjusted, I could discern that it had some type of ornate design along the front. There were several hotel room windows, some of them dark, some of them lit. A revolving door to enter the hotel was illuminated by a tiny light just above where patrons would enter and exit. On either side of the hotel were the same dense bushes that I'd always seen, but I found it quite strange that this old hotel was plopped directly on top of it in the middle of the night. Regardless of how this showed up, I decided I must go down and see for myself.

It was a cool night as I meandered down the hill to check out this hotel. The wind had picked up, and the rustle of the leaves startled me as they swirled along the curbside. I had full intentions of going directly up to the hotel and into it, but once in front, I found it to be larger than I originally thought, and an unnerving feeling came over me as I stopped in the middle of the street directly across from it. I retreated to the rock, sat on it for a moment, and thought about how this large structure came to be.

The concrete face of the building was dark, gray, and aged. It seemed it had been a fancy hotel at one time. There was light coming from inside the front lobby and reception area. I took a deep breath, got up from the rock, and headed across the street toward the revolving door.

The glass door was heavy, but it eventually moved, creaking as it turned to let me in. Inside the lobby, beyond the front desk stood a young man with shiny slicked back black hair. He was in uniform, writing on some paper. I waited there for a moment in the dimly lit lobby with its red cushioned chairs and the mahogany wood along the front desk. To the right was a large wooden staircase leading up to the second floor. There was no one else in the lobby, just the man at the front desk. Behind him were fifteen wooden cubbyholes.

The man eventually raised his head.

"Good evening, sir," he said with a smile

"Good evening."

"Nice to see you again!" It was at this moment that I realized he had a British accent. "Your regular room is free," he said as he turned around to grab the key from cubbyhole number 12. "There you go. Now if you please," He slid the registration slip and ink pen towards me.

I hesitated a moment, wondering how this man would have known me. I hadn't seen him before, and I certainly didn't recall ever coming to this old hotel. He stared at me while I was about to fill out the registration. I decided not to use my name, so I was Mr. John Smith that night!

I filled out the registration and slid the form and pen back to the man at the desk.

He peered down at the slip. "Ahh, very wise . . . Mr. Smith. Do you need assistance with luggage?" he asked as he peeked over the counter.

"No. No bags tonight."

"Have a pleasant evening, Mr. Smith. Welcome back!"

"Thank you!" I said, moving towards the staircase.

I spied from the corner of my eye the man at the front desk watching me as I ascended the curved staircase and eventually left his line of sight. I made it to the landing where a sign displayed rooms 1 to 8 to the left and rooms 9 to 16 to the right. I found my room, slid the key into the door, and opened it. Once inside, I could smell the sweet scent of cologne from the previous occupant. It was a simple room with a bed, an end table, a chair, a closet, and a washroom off to the right.

I placed the key on the end table and sat on the bed, wondering what to do and why I was even there. I was restless. I didn't want to fall asleep yet, but the bed looked inviting. I got up, grabbed the key from the end table, and headed out of my room. I quietly closed the door, so as not to disturb the other tenants.

When the door latched shut, I could hear someone talking in one of the rooms down the hall towards rooms 15 to 16. I turned my head slightly to get a better listen, but I couldn't make out if it was a man's or a woman's voice. I turned in the other direction and continued down the staircase to speak with the man at the front desk.

The man lifted his head as I approached. I asked: "Is there anything here in the hotel that I could read?"

"Having trouble sleeping?" he asked, pointing behind me. "Just over there. You'll find something, I'm sure."

There was a small bookcase with cushioned red chairs on either side. I headed in that direction, the man added, "Pardon me, sir."

"Yes?"

"You have a message," he said, turning around. He reached for a folded note that was tucked into cubbyhole # 12. "This note was left for you shortly after you arrived."

I took it, sat on one of the cushioned chairs, and opened it. Before I started to read, I peeked above it to see the man behind the desk grinning. He eventually turned his eyes back to his desk to write. The note read:

Hello again. I understand you are back. I never sleep, so come by for a visit. I'm in room 9, just down the hall from you.

I folded the paper, placed it in my jacket pocket, and peered up to see the man at the front desk, continuing his writing.

Who could this be? The note was not signed, but this person obviously knew me . . . or was he mistaken? I needed to investigate.

Going towards the staircase, I had to pass the front desk once more, where the man ignored me.

It became clearer to me that this hotel was in bad shape with staining on the ceiling and at the top of the old yellowed walls. I couldn't identify the odor in the hallways, maybe cedar wood.

I made it to room # 9 and stood in front of the door for a moment. I was about to knock when I heard faint voices coming from down the hallway as I did earlier. I turned my attention there.

Passing my room, then passing rooms 13 and 14, I realized it was farther down at the end. The sound came from the room across from 15. There was no number on the door. I heard whispering. I stood in the middle of the hall, with my right ear turned toward the room. I listened as if it were speaking to me. The whispering became intoxicating. I found myself moving towards it without any fear of being caught.

I then surprised myself and moved completely against the door with my ear pressed against it, but the whispering was inaudible. I needed to know what was being said. I then placed my right hand on the handle and the other on the surface to push it open, but as soon as I did, the whispering stopped. I could feel the perspiration collect on my back and under my arms. I let go of the handle and backed away for fear of what was on the other side. Suddenly scared, I continued along the hallway to my room. I took the key out of my pocket and stood in front with the key engaged, while still looking back at the whispering room, but nothing happened; nothing came out. My heart pounded. I'm not sure what came over me. Why was I so willing to enter that room?

I took my key out of the lock and remained in front of my room until my heart stopped palpitating. At room 9, I waited for a moment. I knocked.

"Please enter," said a familiar voice.

I pushed the door open into *complete darkness*.

I let the door shut behind me.

"Hello again, young man," said the voice.

I felt like I had just met up with an old friend.

"Hello," I answered.

The room remained in utter darkness, but it didn't matter.

"You have found yourself in a very interesting place here at this hotel. I understand you've just arrived. I have been expecting you for some time, but I will not keep you long," said the voice. "My reason for having you visit me is quite simple." The voice paused. "You will, no doubt, find yourself invited to a few rooms in the hotel. That is natural. Just know that I am here," the voice reassured me.

A little confused about the comment about being invited to other rooms, I replied: "OK. Thank you!"

I turned around and reached out my arms to feel for the door handle, which I eventually found, and I left the room.

The hallway was blacked out. With the lights off, I could only see a very little amount of light coming from the staircase. I felt around in my pocket to find the key, opened the door, and scratched around the doorframe for the switch to flick the lights, but they didn't turn on either. *The power must be off.* I took in the faint smell of cologne again, which eventually faded.

I backed out of the room, closed the door behind me, and made my way toward the staircase. I didn't realize how creaky the wooden floors were until I made step-by-step movements to avoid tripping.

Once past rooms 9 and 10, I turned towards the staircase where a dim light emitted. Step by step, I made my way down it. The man at the front desk lifted his head, following me the entire time. The right side of his face was lit by an oil lantern.

"I'm afraid we've lost power, Mr. Smith."

"Yes. I noticed."

"Please," the man said "take this with you. It could be out for some time." The man passed me the lantern.

"Thank you."

"Try and enjoy your evening."

The light of the lantern cast my shadow against the staircase and the hallway until I arrived at my room. I unlocked the door and entered. To my surprise, someone was lying in my bed, rolled up under the covers with his back towards me. My first reaction was that I was in the wrong room, so I checked the door; it read 12. I raised my lantern to get a better look. It was a man.

I was irritated.

"Excuse me!" I said and then cleared my throat.

The man turned around and smiled.

"Hello, my twin!" he exclaimed and turned to sit up on the bed.

I approached him with my hand stretched out to shake his. "Good to see you. It's nice to see that one of us is sleeping."

"Haha. Indeed!" He then motioned with his hand toward the chair across from the bed. "Please. Have a seat."

I sat and placed the lantern on the side table. The smell of his sweet cologne was present.

"I knew we would meet again, but I didn't think it would be in this place!" he said as he reached into his suit jacket pocket. He pulled out a pack of cigarettes and banged the box to release one before placing it in his mouth. He searched a few pockets for his lighter, which he eventually found and lit it.

"I didn't know you smoked."

He exhaled.

"I started right after I saw you last. It calms my nerves," he said with the smoke twirling around his neck and face as if it were about to put a snakelike stranglehold on him.

"Tell me something," he said just before taking another drag and exhaling it. "What do you think love is? I mean really . . . what do you think it is . . .

What does it mean to you?" He paused, waving his cigarette. "Before you answer that though; answer this: does it mean that you were in love if your heart aches after a break-up? Or does it simply mean you were heartbroken?"

I studied his face for a moment while I thought about how to answer his question. The light from the lantern gave me a good view for the first time since encountering him again. He seemed tired. It appeared as if he even aged a little. He had dark circles below his eyes, and wrinkles formed on either side when he squinted.

"I'm sure that someone could be heartbroken by someone they hardly knew. In that case, that would be rejection from what I would think would be an infatuation . . . or possibly lust," I offered. "Rejection hurts too. As for your first question . . . what do I think love is?" I said as my twin took another drag. "I believe that love is deep, deep as the experiences we have with that person become intimate, creating a strong bond. That doesn't happen right away. It's an investment of time and energy. That's where the bond begins to build. That would be what I think love is. Once the bond is broken, it hurts. It aches the heart." I thought for a moment. "I suppose that if that bond disintegrates before it's broken suddenly, then there would be less pain . . . or maybe even . . . very little pain at all. There would be no broken heart," I suggested, sitting back in my chair. "Now, here's a question for *you* . . ."

"OK." He took one last drag of his cigarette, blew it, and squished it in the ashtray.

"Is it better to have a bond disintegrate before two lovers' eyes rather than have it severed quickly, causing heartache?" I asked.

My twin reached into his pocket for another cigarette.

"That's a good question. I'd have to think about that one.'" He lit his cigarette and exhaled but kept fixating on the ceiling. "You know . . . Sometimes I think . . . that I think too much."

I didn't say anything, as he was formulating his thoughts while staring upward.

"I think about . . . What is love? Why do we want sex? Why do we *need* sex? Why do we want more things in general. . .? Is living a long life really . . . beneficial?" he asked and then took another drag before flicking the ashes into the tray. "Why do we get angry when things don't go our way? Why do we fight? Why can't we trust everyone? How is it that we can hurt people closest to us?" He shook his head and leaned back with both hands on the edge of the bed. I thought a tear formed in his eye, but I wasn't sure. My twin sat for a moment as he was reflecting on his questions.

The silence was broken by the floor in the hallway creaking. The footsteps stopped, and an envelope slid under it.

"That's for you," he said as he leaned forward in anticipation.

I fetched the envelope. I returned to my seat, opened it, and read it out loud.

Dear neighbor. I understand you have the only means to a lantern in this hotel tonight. I need a little bit of help finding something in the dark. Come by and I'll reward you with a drink.

Room 14

Don't forget that lantern!

My twin lifted his head with his sad eyes and his cigarette smoke swirling around him as he held it below his face.

"Go ahead, I need to catch up on some sleep, anyway," he said as he wrapped himself in blankets and curled up like a little boy trying to fight off the chill.

"Well. I could use a drink. I suppose I'll lend a hand with this lantern," I said, grabbing it.

I lifted the light high to get a better view of the numbers. The '1' on room 14 was crooked. I was about to knock, but before I did, my attention took me farther down the hall. I didn't hear anything at first, which was a bit of a relief, so I turned to face the door again when I heard it. I heard the whisper. It was clearer than it was earlier. I stepped closer. The whispering became louder as I approached. Something kept drawing me to it. I knelt beside the bottom of the door, placing my ear to it. My mind escaped the image of the dank hotel hallway and went somewhere where I shouldn't have - somewhere forbidden. The whispering drew me closer as if I were in a spell. I saw images and experienced the desire to indulge, and lust. I embraced a pleasure that I couldn't entirely relate to. The door to room 14 opened. A middle-aged man appeared.

"Dear boy. What in heaven's name are you doing?" he asked.

"Pardon me, sir. I thought I heard someone call me from beyond the door," I said as I rose.

"Did you not get the note?"

"I did. I was just about to knock on your door when . . ." I said, pointing to the whispering room.

The man seemed quite perturbed.

"Well, come on then! Bring your lantern."

"Yes, sir."

The man rushed towards the staircase but I halted in front of his door. The man turned around.

"I'm going to the lobby to have a cigarette, and I need your light," he said firmly. "Come along"

The man rushed through the hallway and down the staircase as I chased after him with my lantern until we reached the front desk. The concierge was seated, leaning his head against the wall with his eyes closed.

"Wake up!" the man chirped, startling him.

"Yes." The man at the desk responded as he jolted out of his chair.

"I need a match. Do you have one?"

"I do. One moment," he said as he searched through the drawer of his desk. "And here you are."

The man from room 14 leaned forward with the cigarette dangling between his lips, expecting it to be lit for him. I held the lantern high to assist.

"Cheers," the man said pleasantly after exhaling the first puff and headed towards the chairs and bookcase.

The man from room 14 was in his fifties. His thinning hair was salt and pepper, slicked back with pomade. He sported a thin mustache and wore a buttoned-up red cardigan with brown dress pants and black shiny shoes.

"I'm looking for a black cat and have been for some time. He'll have a tiny bell on his collar that likely doesn't ring anymore. If . . ." The man hesitated and then nodded for me to follow him as he took a seat on the red lobby chair. "Once you find him, bring him to me immediately!" He took another drag of his cigarette and exhaled, leaving a cloud of smoke hanging above his head. "On you go!"

"OK."

I thought I'd start with my wing of the hotel and listened for any noises of a cat. No matter how delicately I stepped, the floors were incredibly creaky.

"Hello," said the voice of a woman from the opening of room 14.

"Oh! I'm sorry. . ." I said, startled. "I am trying to be as quiet as I can. . ."

As she held her opened door, the light of my lantern lit up her face. She scanned me up and down for a moment eventually grinning.

"I see you have a lantern. That's very useful on a night like tonight. Come on in."

I hesitated.

"Come in," she repeated.

I entered to view a very nicely decorated room. It was larger than mine and was furnished with two very plush chairs and a love seat; a few candles were burning throughout. The woman reminded me of an actress I once saw in a movie. She wore her blonde hair straight. She possessed very defined facial features, specifically a prominent jawline that I found appealing. She sat on the loveseat across from me.

"Have a seat," she suggested.

I did.

A moment or two passed without anyone speaking.

"The man . . ." I said with a nervous voice, "He said you are missing a cat."

She laughed. "He has been looking for that cat for a very long time." She took a sip from her glass. "Pardon me. I didn't ask if you'd like some wine," and stood. "I'll pour you a glass." She approached a small table beside the bedroom. I took advantage of that moment to observe her figure. The light from the lantern displayed that she had on a long white nightgown and nothing underneath. I enjoyed the image. She presented the wine glass. My hands touched hers slightly as I grabbed it. I took a sip and placed the glass on the round wooden table beside me while she took her seat.

"Thank you!"

"Did you say . . ." I paused as I realized that the woman appeared as if she had something on her mind.

"You were going to say . . ." she prompted.

"Your cat. Your cat has been missing for a very long time?"

"Yes. But you didn't come to look for the cat, did you?" She grinned devilishly.

My immediate reply was going to be a "yes" but that wouldn't have been my true reply.

"No. I suppose not."

"I didn't think so." The woman took a sip.

"Put that light up on the table so I can see you better," she ordered.

I did.

The light allowed me to see the curves of her body underneath her nightgown. She curved her feet as I studied her legs and painted toes.

"Enjoying the view?"

I nodded.

"Anything specifically?"

I swallowed. "Ummm"

"Don't be shy," she said as she got up from her chair and stood in front of me with her legs pressed against mine. "It was me who sent that note. Did you think it was Charles?"

I nodded.

"Charles is a delusional man who keeps using this cat as an excuse to stay with me."

It took everything for me not to reach up and touch her. I was nervous but aroused at the same time as her warm body pressed against mine; her breasts would move up and down with every breath. I wanted nothing more than to touch her. My body shook while aroused at the same time. It was mixed with the fear of being caught by Charles.

"He thinks I'm here looking for his cat," I said, feeling embarrassed how it came out, as I must have sounded like a lost little boy.

"You'll continue, I'm sure," she asserted.

I studied the woman's face as she took me in. I caved into temptation and let my eyes drop to see her breasts and farther down to see her hips as the light from the lantern provided a clear silhouette of her body.

"I must look for that cat," I said disappointed with my own decision.

I stood and gently touched the small of her back when I passed to fetch my lantern.

Once at the door I turned to face the woman.

"I really shouldn't be here," I apologized.

"I think you worry too much."

She stepped closer to me. I could feel her wanting me to touch and kiss her. The physical desire was incredible, but I gained a sudden strength within. Out I went. With my head in a fog as to what had just happened, I took a moment to soak in the magnitude of how much I desired to touch that woman. I felt foolish for walking away from the opportunity that would likely never happen again.

I stopped and placed the lantern on the floor and brought my hand to my forehead as I deliberated as to what I was going to do. Just at that moment, I could hear it: the whisper, coming from the next room. I strode closer and knelt in front of the door. The sound seemed louder nearer the bottom. I needed to hear what it was saying but I couldn't; the whisper took me in, almost sucking me into the room with its inaudible rhythm. I was intoxicated by it, as whatever it was, ran through my blood. My ear was stuck to the door and my right hand pressed against it. From the whisper, I felt an incredible amount of energy enter me. I couldn't hold back the immediate physical need for pleasure. I promptly stood, wiped my face with both hands. I turned and bolted back to room 14. I heard soft footsteps followed by the door opening. I stepped inside, placed both hands on the woman's hips, and backed her against the door. I bunched up her nightgown into my hands, lifting it until I felt her bare skin.

Once I could feel her naked body, I slid my hands up her hips and along her waist. She closed her eyes as my hands continued up to her ribcage. I brought my hands inwards taking her breasts into them. She slid her hands behind my back to bring me closer, but I stopped her. I pulled her nightgown up to her shoulders, holding it up as I leaned down to kiss her breasts. Her eyes closed, enjoying the touch, letting me enjoy her. When I let her nightgown drop, she took my arms in her hands and forced me closer, allowing us to kiss deeply. I brought my hands down along her back until I reached her leg. I lifted it and shoved my right thigh between her legs, causing her body to twist slightly. I dropped her leg. The energy I just felt was being taken over by fear.

"What's wrong?" she asked.

I didn't say anything, as I was still confused by the sudden change I was feeling.

"Are you frightened of him walking in?"

"I am. But not just that. . ." I said as my heart was still pounding. "Is this wrong . . . what we're doing? I don't know what came over me, but I just wanted to touch you. I couldn't help myself." I kept my hand still on her waist. "But I want more of you."

"Then why stop?" she asked, looking a little rejected.

"I don't know."

"Then go. Go look for his silly cat, if that will make you feel better."

The candles weren't bright enough to see the true expression on her face, but I knew she was upset. I wanted her, but the practical side came over me. I wished I could explain this better, but she had already opened the door for me to leave. I entered the hallway, but she didn't close the door entirely.

"I'm not angry at you. I'm just . . . Just go look for that cat. Maybe you can find it!" She closed the door rather loudly.

I picked up the lantern and headed towards my room, but as I was about to place my hand on the door handle, I heard the footsteps of someone coming up the stairs. It was Charles, holding a candle in his left hand.

"Dear boy. Have you had any success?" he inquired.

"Not yet, sir. I'll keep trying."

"Be a good boy and keep looking, will you?" he pleaded as he took out a few bills from his wallet and shoved them into my free hand.

"It's OK. I don't need the money."

"Nonsense! Everyone could use money. In any case, you are the one holding the lantern." He strode past me and onto his room. I turned to mine and placed my hand on the door, but waited. The man placed the key in the door and opened it. "Hello, Darling."

I entered to see my twin still sleeping, so I gingerly placed the lantern on the side table and sat to stretch my legs. My twin rustled with the sheets and turned around.

"Hello!" He yawned and sat up on his bed. He rubbed his face with his hands and leaned forward to reach for his cigarette box that was on the side table. The light showed his face clearer now. I tried to conceal my surprised look as I realized he had aged even more since before he went to sleep. His hair was beginning to gray and it was thinning. Lines had formed around his mouth and nose.

"Care to tell me about your visit?" he asked with a grin while trying to bang out a cigarette from its box.

I sat in shock over how my twin had aged so quickly. I was about to say something, but I pushed down the impulse. I switched my thoughts to my adventure in room 14 and then to Charles and the missing cat.

"Oh, yes. The missing cat. I didn't find it."

"No. I didn't think so. Maybe you found something else," he insinuated, lighting his cigarette. "You know . . ." he said letting out his first puff. ". . . I've been thinking more about our earlier conversation. What keeps a man and a woman together? Is it strictly love?" He paused. "Oh, I know there are many loveless relationships out there. They stay together for money, security, fear of loneliness, etc., etc.," he said, waving his cigarette. "I think you are right." He took another drag. "It is a bond. Sex and passion are a part of it, but the bond they build keeps them together. Sex and passion are beautiful, but it's short-lived by itself, I suppose." He sat for a moment while I listened. He scratched his head with the same hand he held his cigarette. "The heartache I had when we last met . . . it's going away." He took another drag. "The heartbreak is going away and it's kind of sad because . . . when there was heartache, there had to be passion, and without either, I barely feel alive. Having said that . . . I feel a sort of . . . peace within me. I feel content. I'm not used to contentment. I'll have to admit, it scares me a little. I'm not sure I love it." He put out his cigarette. "What are you going to do with that money Charles gave you?"

"I don't know. I don't want it, but I can't just throw it away. Perhaps I should keep searching for that cat, then I'll feel better."

"Oh, my twin, my twin. You are too practical for your own good!"

"Well. I'm going to try and have another look." I felt quite guilty for how I handled myself in room 14. "What will you do?" I asked, getting up.

"I'm tired. I'm going to take a shot of whiskey and get some sleep. I didn't sleep well earlier." He opened the top drawer of the end table to pull out a bottle of whiskey and a small glass. He pulled out the cork, poured a shot, and tilted his head back to take it. He climbed into bed and rolled back over to have another nap.

I grabbed the lantern and let myself out, closing the door quietly behind me. I continued towards the staircase to the other side of the hall, at which point I crossed paths with a hotel worker who was bringing something from the other wing of the hotel down towards the stairs.

I greeted him.

"Good evening," he replied as he passed me.

The hotel worker was in a gray and blue uniform and appeared to be bringing two large bags of garbage downstairs with him. He was a middle-aged man with blond hair that was parted on one side.

"Have you, by any chance, seen a black cat wandering around the hallway?" I asked.

The man stopped for a moment as he took his first step down the stairs.

"Yes, but it's been a while." He paused. "I've seen him near the garbage disposal. Come on down with me. You can look down there for the cat." I followed the man down the stairs, with my lantern raised high so that he could see where he was going.

"By the way." The man half-turned as he kept walking.

"Yes?"

"What room are you in?"

"I'm in room 12," I replied

The man stopped. "Room 12? What are you doing in that wing of the hotel? That side hasn't been in service for years!" He studied me for a moment. "I figured you were just walking around." He regained his pace until he stopped in front of the maintenance room. "Is it even clean?"

"Yes. It's fine."

He set down the two bags. "You don't know the story about room 15?"

"No."

The man leaned his back up against the wall.

"Well. Then, I must tell you. About twenty years ago, there was a Swedish scientist who stayed in that room for several months. I was a young man at the time working as a bellboy. The scientist had developed a potion. The potion, as it were, was dubbed "Utopia." It was apparently very potent, as all you needed was one drop on your tongue and you felt as if you were in Utopia for three to four hours. The scientist's original intent was to sell it to hospitals for the pure reason of giving it to patients who were dying rather than the painkillers that were prescribed at the time. He only brought three little bottles with him as two of the ingredients were from rare plants: one from Madagascar and one from Western Australia. He was originally to come with a man: a Swedish businessman. This Swedish businessman was to introduce the scientist to some investors, but he became ill and died a few weeks before they were to board the ship to North America. The scientist was certainly not a businessman and ended up taking on the responsibility of meeting with investors himself, which he was not very good at, as you'll hear shortly. The investors that showed interest did not, however, work for hospitals; they had . . ." He paused. ". . . other intentions. The scientist became tired of meeting with these investors as they were not showing enough serious intent or were unable to secure proper funding. After time had passed and there was little interest from serious investors, the scientist kept to himself until his train was ready to depart so that he could board his ship to return home. During one of his last full days before leaving, the scientist was approached in the hotel by a man who seemed genuinely interested in the Utopia potion. This discussion took place in the lobby as I was there and witnessed the entire interaction," the man said, staring up at the ceiling, as the memory seemed to play out in his head.

"This investor, whose name I can't recall, was interested in the potion, but wanted to buy the formula outright, and the scientist refused. The scientist was genuinely insulted, said something in Swedish, and off he went to his room. The scientist then became paranoid because of this would-be-investor and quickly returned to the lobby to see if this man had left the hotel, but he hadn't. The investor checked into room 11; directly across from you. Furthermore, after a telegram was sent by the man in room 11, a business acquaintance of his came late that evening and stayed in room 10. I remember *his* name. It was Charles."

I opened my mouth as I was just about to say that I'd met the man but closed it and listened. "The story is that the scientist became worried about these two men and took some precautions. First; he hid his three bottles of Utopia. Secondly; that cat that you are searching for?" the man said, turning his head towards me. "That cat contained the formula. I'll get to that part in a minute. That night, the would-be investor broke into the scientist's room and found two of the three bottles, but he overdosed from it while still in his room. The next morning, the local police arrived to investigate the dead man in room 11. The scientist was interrogated by the police, but no bottles were found in his possession or in his room. The next day he carried on his way to Sweden." He paused for a moment.

"The story doesn't end there though," he continued. "Now, here is the story of the cat. The cat was a stray that the scientist took a liking to while he held residence here at the hotel. Every day the black cat would come by and greet the scientist, so the scientist would feed him a treat. He enjoyed the company of this cat and somehow affixed a little bell on its collar so that the scientist could hear him coming." The man paused for a moment. "As to how the cat got the formula, well; on the night the scientist hid the three bottles, he wrote the formula on a very tiny piece of paper. He folded it and tucked it into the cat's bell with the intent of taking the pet with him on his trip back to Sweden when the time came, but the cat could not be found on the day of his departure. The scientist left with no formula and no bottles of Utopia. Charles stayed in every room in that wing looking for the last bottle of potion and the cat, but he didn't and eventually went bankrupt and died of a stroke in room 14. That was the last I heard of the Utopian potion. The hotel closed that wing after Charles died. I don't know why really. The owner never explained, but I have my suspicions," he said, sighing.

I reached into my pocket to confirm if the paper money was still there. It was.

"Was there ever a woman that stayed with Charles in room 14?" I asked sheepishly.

"Oh? Have you seen her?" he asked, surprised and then a little concerned as if he had more to tell me.

"I've met her."

"You met her?" he exclaimed. He took a step closer and looked at me as if he were about to poke me to see if I was a ghost. He backed away, looking uncomfortable.

"To be honest . . ." he said, picking up the garbage bags again. ". . . that wing frightens me. You won't see me down there for any reason. Besides, the tenants in the other wing keep me busy. They keep me very busy." He continued through the maintenance room and past the boiler.

"I really don't know how you ended up getting a room in that wing," he said.

He dropped the one bag again, opened another door, which was to the outside. He then flung the two bags onto a large mound of trash and wiped his hands on his pants.

"There you go. That's where I last saw the cat . . . twenty years ago," he decreed with a grin.

I looked back at the man, speechless, as I felt completely foolish. *That cat is long gone now.* I almost turned back until I saw the garbage pile that the man threw the two bags on was larger than I had first imagined. I raised my lantern higher to get a better view and continued towards it. The pile of garbage went as far as I could see. I've never seen so much of it. I turned to the man.

"This hotel produces this much garbage?" I was in complete shock.

The man nodded. "They all come looking for the cat, or at least the bell with the formula . . . and the bottle, of course. This is what they produce. Good luck finding the cat. He may still be around. You never know. Stranger things have happened."

The man went back inside and closed the door. I turned around to find myself between two very long mountains of garbage. These went on and on until I lost sight of the end of it. The mounds were at least ten feet over my head. I continued walking and walking and at times would take a closer view of what this garbage consisted of. Everything was in it! I saw packaging and apple cores and old shoes, pants, umbrellas, gum wrappers, cigarette butts, pop bottles, rum bottles, and postcards; the list went on and on. I must have walked a mile or two at this point.

As I continued, the story of the cat and the formula came to mind. *Now I can appreciate why Charles and all the tenants in the other wing of the hotel are looking for this cat. It must be worth a fortune! Now I need to find it for myself!* I called and whistled for it; anything that would get its attention. I continued for what seemed like hours, but I eventually felt exhausted to the point where I thought I heard the tinkle of a bell in the distance. I continued for some time until I completely lost sight of the hotel, at which point I decided to turn around and return in defeat. Mile after mile I hiked between the two enormous piles. I couldn't see the hotel but instead the garbage pile slowly closing in. I held the lantern high to view that I was surrounded by garbage at which point I collapsed to my knees with the lantern almost tipping over. I sat still mentally exhausted -- I *really should be sleeping right now rather than looking for a cat. Why don't I see anyone else looking for it?*

I sat in the middle of the mounds of garbage, wondering what to do. *Do I dig my way out? Do I try and climb over? Yes, that's it! I'll climb over it.* I took a few steps towards the mound and then took a big step onto the garbage, but my foot slipped and fell forward but gained my footing. I took a few steps back from the mound and ran towards it, taking a few larger leaps but didn't gain any traction and kept slipping down the mound, almost dropping the lantern while getting the remnants of garbage on my clothes as I fell flat on my stomach.

"Dammit!" I said as I could smell the putrid odor of the trash.

I stood in the middle for a moment with the lantern in my hand, gazing up at the sky, wondering how I was going to get out of this situation. I placed the lantern on the ground, knelt, crossed my legs, and sat. I began to get angry with myself as to why I was so focused on finding this cat. I had been here for so long strategizing as to how I was to escape, then wanting to kick myself for being in this position. I felt disgusted with all this garbage stuck to me. *The predicaments I get myself into.*

Although feeling poorly because of the situation I was in, I was still intrigued about the cat, the formula, and the missing bottle of Utopia that was somewhere in that hotel. I thought *I could certainly use a drop of Utopia right about now. This is certainly humbling.* I continued to sit with my legs crossed, my elbows on my knees, and the palms of my hands wrapped around my jaw, closing my eyes every once in a while, until I heard a clanking sound as if someone was banging a pipe. The noise came from beyond the garbage, then stopped. A few minutes later, I heard it again, this time a little closer. It stopped. I heard it one last time almost directly below. I got up onto my hands and knees and yelled down toward where the sound was coming from.

"Hello!"

"Hello up there!" I heard a faint voice from below. "Can you hear me?" the voice asked a little louder. The voice was of a man with an English accent. "Clear the dirt away." The voice said, so I put the lantern aside and began to push the dirt away from directly where the voice was coming from. I kept on for a few minutes but wasn't making any progress, so I looked into the garbage pile to find a wooden stick to break up the dirt until I discovered a metal manhole cover.

"Hold on! Almost there."

I pushed the dirt away until it was completely clear. I jammed the stick in the hole of the manhole cover to prop it open, which it did, and slipped off the stick and banged back down. I tried this a few times to no avail.

"Wait!" I heard from below.

The cover moved then lifted slightly, under which were two hands pushing the metal cover to one side. Out came the head of the man from the front desk. He looked around, rather silly with his head turning around as it stuck out from the manhole.

"My goodness! You got yourself in quite a pickle!" he stated. "Come on down. We'll get you back to your room in no time."

"Thank you!" I was curious as to why he said: "we."

I handed him the lantern and then turned around and climbed down the manhole. With the British concierge was an old man. He was severely hunched holding a candle. Both men stood on one side of the sewer as dirty water flowed in the middle. The water was foul-smelling, causing me to plug my nose. The old man walked ahead of us. The man from the front desk handed me the lantern and continued following behind the old man.

"We've been looking for you for some time," said the man with the accent.

"Oh?"

"Your friend here came looking for you, so I thought I'd try this route since the garbage shifted a little while ago."

As I carefully made my steps, I asked myself who this old man was. *I don't recall seeing a man that old in the hotel. It's not Charles. Who could it be?*

As we continued, I felt moisture dripping onto my head and shoulders, causing me to look up. I lifted the lantern to have a better view of the sewer tunnel ceiling and the moisture forming at its brim. My foot slipped and I landed in the middle of the stream of putrid water, still holding the lantern. The man from the front desk bent over and took the lantern, passed it to the old man, and reached his hand to mine. I was now soaked with contaminated water consisting of everything including human waste. I began to gag and vomit as the odor was so strong, but nothing came up except bile as I had nothing in my stomach for hours.

"Come on old chap," said the man from the front desk. "Let's get you to your room."

We walked and walked for another mile or so until we reached the end of the sewer tunnel, where the old man was helped up the ladder with the assistance of the concierge. I witnessed the old man shake as he strained to take each step. Once up, I discovered that we were back in the maintenance room of the hotel, beside the boiler.

"I'll take him to his room and get him cleaned up," said the old man with a scratchy voice.

"Cheers!' the man from the front desk called and turned to head back to the front.

I followed the man holding the lantern as he shuffled through the lobby and up the stairs. While he pushed the key into the door, I scanned the hallway. Many of the doors were open. Rooms 10 and 11 and even room 14 were all left open. I passed the old man, focusing my attention on room 14. I needed to know why.

"Hello!" I called.

Nothing.

I continued in. The room was abandoned and filled with cobwebs and dust. *No one had been here for years!*

"Let's get you out of those clothes," the old man called from my room. I followed him feeling utterly drained. My disappointment didn't end there. It was at that moment that I realized my twin had left. The bed covers were left scattered amongst the bed. I needed to talk to him about everything that just happened. *Perhaps he is in the lobby. I will check on him after I clean up.*

The old man placed the lantern and key on the side table.

"Take those off and go take a shower. I have some clothes put aside for you. They don't fit me anymore," said the old man as he turned away from me. I stripped down and threw my clothes in a bundle in the corner of the bathroom in disgust. I washed off the film and grease and smell until I felt clean once again. I grabbed a towel to dry off and dressed in the old man's clothes. To my surprise, they fit perfectly. They even resembled the clothes I once wore. At that very moment, dread came over me. I moved towards the old man, who sat on the bed hunched over, peering at the ground. I leaned in to gain a better view.

"My twin?" I asked.

The old man slowly raised his head, his eyes finally meeting mine. Yes. Those are the eyes of my twin.

"Yes, my twin," he said in his tired scratchy voice. "It's me. You were gone a very long time. I waited for you, but you didn't come."

I could feel tears form in my eyes, but I forced them down. My twin was now in the body of an eighty-year-old man. His white hair was very thin with age spots on the top of his head. His eyes were sunken in as well as the skin on his cheeks. His lips were very dry and cracked and the skin on his neck was loose and looked as if it were barely hanging on. His hands were boney and shaky. I had to look away to avoid staring.

"I take it . . ." he said, catching his breath, "that you never found the cat."

"No," I replied. "You must be tired after walking that tunnel."

He didn't answer but nodded.

"Thank you for the clothes," I said. "Are you going to rest some more?"

"I think I will. I'm not feeling very well." He took another breath. "Are you going to look for that potion?" he asked, while still sitting on the bed.

"I think I will. I don't think I'll ever find the cat."

He pointed to his legs. "Can you help me with these?"

I leaned over to bring his legs up and onto the bed. "Better?" I queried.

"Thank you." He replied as his scratchy voice began to fade from exhaustion. He then murmured something.

"I didn't hear you," I said, wanting to.

"I said." He then cleared his throat. "The ache is gone. The heartache. It's all gone. I am very sad." He then muttered something again and closed his eyes.

"Sleep well." I grabbed the lantern and closed the door behind me.

I went to room 15. Once in front, I placed my hand on the door handle but didn't turn it; instead, I waited . . . I waited to convince myself this was a good idea when I heard it again. I heard the whisper. It was calling me from across the hall. I turned my head and within moments, the lantern was placed on the ground, and my ear was pushed up against the door. The whisper was very clear. I felt it. I heard it. It spoke directly to me. It was very decisive that night. I stood instantly, grabbed the lantern, veered directly to room 13, and opened the door. The room was old and dingy and had a sour odor to it. There was a dirty mattress on a metal bed frame. The lantern cast my shadow onto the stark walls, veiled in cobwebs. I knew exactly where I was going though. I approached the closet, crouched, and felt around the inside of it. I tore off a small piece of baseboard and reached in with my fingers until I felt it. A large smile stretched across my face.

I had it.

I got the potion!

I brought the tiny bottle back around so I could see it as I held it up to the lantern. The bottle was full.

I found my way to the bathroom, my hands shaking with anticipation of what I discovered. I placed the lantern on the floor so that I could hold the tiny bottle in my left hand while I unscrewed the dropper with my right. I took some deep breaths until my hand steadied. I pulled the dropper out and placed it back in. I squeezed it and pulled it up high so that I could see the color of the fluid within the tube. The fluid slid down, forming a drop. I studied it as it grew larger at the end of the tube.

I opened my mouth, sticking my tongue out, letting the drop splash onto it. I closed my mouth, savoring every bit. I inserted the dropper back in the tiny bottle, screwed it on, and placed the bottle onto the side of the sink.

I waited for a moment and nothing happened. Maybe the formula had lost its strength. Maybe it was all used up and filled with water. *No. That can't be.* The taste was unique. It tasted like something tropical with a slightly sour aftertaste.

I grew impatient and walked back to the hallway with the lantern. I leaned against the wall between rooms 13 and 15, waiting for something to happen.

Then it hit me.

It hit me really hard! So much so, that I fell to my elbow and forearm to avoid banging my head. I was overcome by true bliss. It felt wonderful. It was as if nothing could hurt me emotionally or physically. I was invincible in every form. It was like I was going one hundred miles an hour with no barriers. I was flying. I was free, so free, so peaceful, no pain . . . no pain, nothing to worry me, nothing . . . nothing at all. Time was gone. I didn't care about anything. . . I then grew very, very tired. So very tired.

I lifted my head out of my arms to see the bright light of the lantern. The light was so intense that I squinted and blocked its penetration with my hand to allow my eyes to adjust. I have no idea how long I had been lying there or what had happened to me. I scratched my head and rubbed my eyes. I closed them again to recollect the Utopian state I just experienced. I thought about how beautiful it was.

I observed door 13 and then the whispering room and back to room 13. I felt something; it was the after-effects of the potion and the instant desire to return there. I wanted to taste that distinct flavor of the formula on my tongue once more. I needed to experience that numb state of bliss again and it was right there, in that room, only a drop away. I sat up and licked my lips, tasting the remnants of what I had taken earlier. The blood in my veins trembled shortly after with delight. That's how powerful it was!

I heard it again. I heard it right across from me. It was one whisper. It took one very soft whisper and up I went to room 13 -- directly to the bathroom. I wasted no time unscrewing the bottle top and squeezing the dropper. My tongue was already out before the dropper was pulled from the bottle. I held it high over my mouth. I suddenly pulled my arm away. The drop couldn't hold on any longer and splashed to the floor beside my right shoe. I studied the drop as it was absorbed by the floorboards. I considered the bottle. I stood there holding the dropper for a minute, then slowly closed it screwing the top back on tightly. I felt the need to place the bottle back where it was hidden, placing the baseboard back over it. I closed the closet door, grabbed the lantern, and left room 13.

While still in front, holding the lantern, the reflection of the light was shaking. My hand shook uncontrollably. I leaned back against the wall and slid down to the ground. I studied my hand as it shook. I grabbed it with my other to steady it, then placed both hands over my face to cover the tears as they rolled down my cheeks and chin. I wiped my eyes and cheeks and took a couple of deep breaths until I had enough strength to get back up

After a few minutes passed, I regained the lantern and retreated to my room to see how my twin was doing. I entered, being sure not to wake him. My twin was nicely tucked under his covers with his eyes closed. I placed the lantern on the end table and sat on the bed beside him. He looked very frail. I was gone longer than I thought. He was now almost skin and bones. His mouth was open so that he could breathe. His left arm was not covered by the blanket which showed how skeleton-like it was. I could see that my twin had very little time left. I shifted a little on the bed, causing him to open his eyes. He closed them again and brought his bony hand against mine to show me that he knew I was there. I watched as my twin's chest moved in and out slowly as he breathed. I placed my right hand on his boney little face.

"I didn't take the second drop. It was close, but I didn't do it," I said, tearing up.

His mouth moved to try to say something, but I could tell it was too difficult for him to talk. I knew the heartache was completely gone now. I sat with my hand on his face, watching his breathing change each time he took a breath.

"It's OK. It's all gone now," I said, comforting him.

He didn't respond but his breathing slowed.

I sat with him for quite some time. As time passed, so did his ability to breathe. The longer I watched, the slower his breathing became. It slowed until there were large gaps between each breath until he took one last breath in and after a moment, let it out. I left my hand on his face and brought the other up to place it on his hand and watched how life left my twin's body. I sat studying his face and body: so tiny and lifeless. I drew the blanket up to his neck and tucked his arm underneath. I brushed his thin white hair away from his face with my hand, then I got up, grabbed the lantern, and left my room. I stopped in the hallway for a moment, taking in the strange ambiance. I didn't feel the pull of the whispering room, so I left and carried on down the staircase to the front desk where I thanked the man for all his help, passed over the lantern, and checked out of the hotel.

I crossed the street to the rock. I turned around to have one last look at the old hotel and then made my way up the hill, into my house, and into my bedroom. I undressed and slid under the covers. I closed my eyes and placed my head on the pillow.

Tick, tick, tick, tick, tick, tick . . .

The End

Manufactured by Amazon.ca
Bolton, ON